A
Gay S... 's

First Edition

Published by The Nazca Plains Corporation
Las Vegas, Nevada
2009

ISBN: 978-1-935509-19-6

Published by

The Nazca Plains Corporation ®
4640 Paradise Rd, Suite 141
Las Vegas NV 89109-8000

© 2009 by The Nazca Plains Corporation. All rights reserved.
No part of this work may be reproduced or utilized in any form or by any means, electronic or mechanical, including photocopying, microfilm, and recording, or by any information storage and retrieval system, without permission in writing from the publisher. Printed in the United States of America.

PUBLISHER'S NOTE
A Gay Sailor's Journey is a work of fiction created wholly by *Wayne Telfer'*s imagination. All characters are fictional and any resemblance to any persons living or deceased is purely by accident. No portion of this book reflects any real person or events.

Cover Photo, Jose Barrera
Art Director, Blake Stephens

Dedication

This is dedicated to all those military men who have been able to make a success of their military time while having to conceal their homosexuality. Gay man can, after all, serve and fight too.

A
Gay Sailor's Journey

First Edition

Wayne Telfer

A Gay Sailor's Journey

Emmett rang up yet another round of bowling. It was actually a quiet day at the alley. But then it was the middle of the week, so there wasn't much traffic in and out, even if it was the beginning of summer. The kids usually didn't start hanging out at the alley until a few weeks after school; too many 'opening of summer vacation' sort of things to do. However, a few old timers did come in to practice. Of course, Emmett knew most of them. He'd been bowling at these lanes since he was ten. Now that he was nineteen, he'd been bowling in the adult leagues for nearly two years. It was a lot of fun working here now. It gave him the chance to banter with the patrons outside of the league.

For most people, working at a bowling alley might seem like a pretty dreary job. But Emmett liked it because besides working the front counter, he was also qualified to perform all the maintenance on the machines. That meant that he was never sure from one day to the next if he'd be working up front at the register or in back, keeping the machines running. Hell, there was even the occasional day when he was doing both. That always kept him hopping.

Today was a nice mid-week day. It was a Wednesday, with two of them working, and very few patrons. That made for a quiet day with time for the maintenance guy to work on a couple of the troublesome machines. Emmett looked over the rental shoes and fixed or discarded them, and then roamed around the alleys, fixing small problems, emptying ashtrays, and picking up a bit of occasional trash.

He wasn't making as much money as he had during the school year, but it paid his limited bills, being as how he was still living at home. At least he was for another couple of months. He'd be leaving in a couple of months to attend Navy boot camp. July seventeenth was the magical day. But he missed his bus driving job.

He'd spent the last six months driving a school bus and had really enjoyed the fun, and especially the money. But school was out and there wasn't much call for school buses in the summer. There were drivers with more seniority that got the summer work, so Emmett had taken this job to fill in the time until he left for his new life.

The Navy. He'd given the idea a lot of thought before he'd signed on. The education was why he'd really done it. His parents just could not afford to send him to college. So he'd thought that maybe a military stint might fill the bill. But he had worries too. Just how would it work out for him?

He was a nineteen year old gay boy and he was about to immerse himself into a society of primarily male bodies. Would he be able to cope? Would he be able to somehow meet other gay guys and make it work? Of course, he was only obligated to six years. A bit long as enlistments went, but he'd qualified for Nuclear Trained Electronics Technician and that required a longer hitch.

Emmett was just finishing up his work with the shoes when the phone rang and it was his Navy recruiter on the other end.

"Hey, Emmett."

"Hi ya, Chief Martins. Let me guess, they're so short handed that the Navy wants me tomorrow."

They laughed, but Emmett noticed that there was a bit of hesitation in the Chief's response.

"Actually, Emmett, there's been a typically military snafu. It seems your application for the Nuclear Power School came in at the end of a long line of other applications and their original school date for you is already full. What that means is that we're going to have to delay your enlistment for another two months. You're now slated to begin boot camp on September tenth."

"Is this some of that 'hurry up and wait' you told me about, Chief?"

Now Chief Martins did laugh. "I'm afraid so, Emmett."

"Well, it's not like there's anything we can do about it. Do I need to come in and sign some more papers?"

"No, no. You can simply stop by anytime you have a free moment and I'll give you a copy of the new schedule."

Well, that had been a surprise. Another two months of herding bowlers around the place. But it also meant he'd be able to enjoy the whole summer at home with people he knew before being sent off to regions unknown with strangers. That could be good…or bad. All this change was a little frightening, to be sure. Emmett always seemed to have just a bit of a queasy feeling any time he thought about his near future. He'd spent nineteen years simply being your typical kid growing up. Now he was planning to take a giant leap into adulthood; and it was going to be all on his own. None of the close parental support he'd had all these years.

It'd also be without any romantic support. He and Theison had been a couple for the last two years, until Theison had moved to Montana to work on his uncle's ranch. Emmett had been invited to come alone but… ranching? No, that was *not* his cup of tea. He and Theison had been sexually involved for two years, but fortunately it had never turned into a true romance. Still, Emmett missed him. His hand would get the job done, but nothing like Theison had been able to do.

It wouldn't have been so bad, but this small town just did not warrant a gay community. There were no openly gay men or boys anywhere that Emmett could discover. In fact, learning about Theison had been a singularly miraculous event.

It had been a chilly October afternoon two years ago, their senior year of high school. Emmett had headed out from school for the walk home, when he'd discovered Theison walking just ahead of him, going in the same direction. He'd called out, recognizing him as the new boy in town. They'd made the walk home together. By the time Theison had to turn away for his home, Emmett and he had struck up a comfortable friendship. They had no classes together, but they walked to and from school together from that day forward.

It'd been a month later on the walk home that everything changed between them. It was a monumentally miserable walk home. There was a massive snow storm in progress. They could barely see five feet in front of themselves. They were just passing the only park in town when they both decided that they'd had enough and needed to take some shelter until the snow fall let up a bit. They'd retreated to the public restroom.

Even if the restroom wasn't heated, still, the fact that it had been all closed up had maintained the internal temperature significantly warmer than the outdoors. So they'd shed their snow covered coats and brushed off the clinging snow from their pants and hair and had sat down on the floor as far from the entrance as they could. They'd both stretched out to allow their pants to dry as best they could. Well, this left all their assets, covered though they were, out there for everyone to see.

Emmett had been the first to start reacting to the presence of this handsome boy beside him. After all Theison wasn't gorgeous or Adonis material, but he was mildly handsome. He was five-ten or so, couldn't have weighed much less than Emmett, who weighed one hundred and sixty-five pounds, but stood six feet even. They both had dark brown hair. Theison's was cut short, while Emmett let his grow a bit below his ears. Both boys had brown eyes and their complexions were clear.

What Emmett liked most about Theison was his sense of humor. He was the best at discovering something humorous in almost any situation. It'd given them both many hours of delight, simply laughing at some school day occurrence, as they reminisced about the day on their way home. This little interlude in the restroom really was the first time they'd stopped and just sat together. For some reason, they'd never gotten up the nerve to visit each other.

So here they were, two stranded eighteen year olds, all alone in a public restroom, sitting so close that they could feel the heat from the other. Emmett's reaction to their closeness had not been meteoric, but it had been steady and obvious. His thick, eight and a half inches always rested horizontally to the left and so the growing bulge was not something that could be easily hidden, especially since they'd both pulled their pant's legs down to smooth out the material in the hopes of them drying faster.

Emmett became immediately embarrassed and a bit worried, but he dare not move to adjust himself or he'd only bring attention to his nearly full blown woody. He could only hope that Theison was not one of those that tended to glance at his neighbors crotch. But, of course, no such luck.

"So, is that a banana in your pocket, or are you just happy to see me?" asked Theison.

Emmett had blushed the deepest red, but couldn't seem to find his voice. Damn it, why did this always have to happen? He really liked Theison, as a friend, and had hoped that their friendship would continue to grow. Now, that would all be history because he simply could not control his natural reaction to being close to a handsome guy.

"Hey, don't sweat it, Em. I got one too." Theison scooted down a bit so that his woody was more in evidence. "My banana doesn't look as big as yours, but it's there."

And yes, there it was. Theison was right, too. The bulge in his pants wasn't quite as big as Emmett's but that hardly mattered to him. He'd never been a size queen.

"So, what d'ya think? Should we come out to each other?" asked Theison.

Typical Theison. Find the humorous way to approach a delicate subject.

"I guess it'd be sort of hard to deny this," said Emmett, pointing to his bulge. He then looked up into Theison's eyes and saw no ridicule, no condemnation. What he saw was interest. "I really like you, Theison."

The other boy had laughed at that. "Duh, ya think?" Then he'd laughed at his own jest. It took him a moment or two to recover. "Why don't you call me Ty, Em. That's what I like my guys to call me."

"Guys?"

"Ok, so there've only been a couple over the last few years. No one here, though. At least 'til now. What d'ya think, Em, wanna be 'guys'?"

"Yeah, Ty, I'd like us to be 'guys'."

"Ever done anything with another boy?" asked Ty.

"Just like you, I suppose. A couple of guys ever since puberty. One was an adult that taught me."

"Yeah, me too. So, think we'd be safe to have a bit of fun… just to keep us warm, you understand?"

They'd proceeded to undo each others' pants and give the other a blow job. Neither of them lasted too long, and it was over much too quickly for either of them, but it had been a very enjoyable and unexpected beginning.

They'd hit it off immediately. They were very compatible lovers and had taken thorough advantage of their two year association. They'd had as much fun coming up with locales where they could have their sexual fun as they had with the actual acts. They'd thoroughly explored every facet of their sexuality during that time. Emmett, it turned out, was much more comfortable on the bottom, but could switch hit when Ty had wanted his occasional itch scratched.

Their separation had not been a big boo-hoo affair. Both knew they'd miss the other for a time, but they had never felt compelled to take their relationship further than the sex. So they'd parted friends, promising to stay in touch. And they had. Emmett had gotten a new letter from Ty just yesterday, in fact. He went on and on about the huge cocks at the ranch. Then, of course, he'd clarified himself by saying that he'd been referring to the horses.

That little reminiscence brought a smile to Emmett as he got his latest customer set up with shoes and a pair of lanes to bowl on. Just as the man left the counter, the phone rang yet again.

"Emmett, this is Joe Adams."

Well, there was an unexpected surprise. Joe was the dispatcher for the bus company Emmett had worked for. He was a pleasant sort of guy, always cheerful in the mornings when the drivers were just arriving, still much too sleepy.

"Joe, what a surprise. So, what can the bowling alley do for you today?"

"Actually, nothing. I'm calling to talk to you. We've got a bit of a situation here at the company and I think you can help us sort it out. But it's not something I'm comfortable talking about over the phone. I was wondering if you could possibly take an hour off for lunch or something so that we could talk. I'd come pick you up and we could go to my place and I'll order in a pizza."

Emmett checked with the boss, who happened to be in house taking care of paperwork, and it was arranged. Emmett would take a one hour lunch at one o'clock.

When Emmett exited the bowling alley, Joe was sitting just outside in his old dilapidated station wagon.

"God's Joe, haven't seen something like this in like forever."

"It was my parents' car when I was growing up. It needs some exterior work, but I've got the engine and interior up to factory specs."

And it was true. The engine purred. There was no hint that it was anything but in perfect running condition. The interior was equally fine. It looked to Emmett like it had just come from the factory. It even had a bit of that new car smell to it.

"Been working on this for two years now. I'm going to get the body work done next month. Then she'll be good as new."

"Must've been a lot of work."

"Yeah, but it's been worth it to me. I always loved this old car. Dad's amazed that I'm taking all the time and money to fix her up, but I think he's secretly thrilled too. Keeps asking me when it'll be done. I think he wants to take it for a spin, for ole time's sake."

They laughed at this.

Joe lived in one of the finer apartment complexes in town. He parked outside the building and showed Emmett into the apartment. It was actually a well appointed and decorated place.

"Gees, Joe, this looks like something out of Better Homes and Gardens."

"Thanks. I've done it all myself. Most of it's been done on a K-Mart budget though."

"You're kidding. It sure doesn't look like it. And you've done this all yourself?"

"Every bit of it. So, why don't we sit at the bar and I'll order a pizza and we can get down to business."

The bar was the breakfast bar, of course. Joe pulled out a soda for each of them and then ordered a supreme pizza to be delivered in thirty minutes. Then he began explaining the company problem.

"You know we've got the contract for the shuttle on the army base, right?" Emmett nodded. "Well, we've had complaints that the driver doesn't seem to be all there most nights. What we're worried about is drugs. Our preliminary investigation leads us to believe that, if he's not actually selling drugs, he's at least smoking on the job. That's a safety risk and a big liability issue for the company."

"I can certainly see that."

"Well, I suggested that we should try to get someone to ride the shuttle for a few nights. Someone young that might be thought of as a 'cool dude'. I immediately thought of you. You see, this guy was always one of our late shift drivers during the school year. You never ran across each other. But he's been with us an awful long time and I don't want to can him on circumstantial evidence.

"The owner has guaranteed you full wages, at your field trip rate, while you're riding and investigating this."

Well that was a concession. Drivers made good wages. But if you were given a field trip, you got double time while driving and time and a half if you had to sit and wait for a return trip.

"Driving or waiting?"

Joe smiled. "I told them you'd be quick enough to ask. They've authorized the driving rate for this, Emmett. It's that important to them."

"Which shift?"

"He drives the six to midnight shift. Would that fit into your current work schedule?"

"That wouldn't be a problem. My day ends at five."

"Great! So I thought that you could just get on and off at various locations and stay an hour or so and just get known as being a new regular. You may see something, you may not. But you're more likely to see something than anyone else I can think of. You're just out of high school, so you still have that school boy look to you."

'Well, you know I can use the money. Especially money like you're offering. So, you want me to do this for a week?"

"At first. We may ask you to do a second, depending on what you notice."

"Okay, I'm your man, then." And they shook on it. It was just a touch unusual, because this seemed to be a lingering shake.

"So, Emmett," said Joe as he released his hand, "Going off to boot camp pretty soon, aren't you?"

Emmett laughed. "Funny you should bring that up. Got a call from the recruiter today telling me my enlistment has been delayed until the middle of September because of school availability."

"That's too bad. I know you were looking forward to going."

Emmett smiled. "Yeah, mostly. It's a little scary too."

Joe laughed. "I know how that is. I was scared to death when I left for Navy boot camp."

"You were in the Navy?"

"Uh huh. I did four years when I was your age. I was a Boson's Mate. Not much for gaining skills, but it got me away from home and I got to see a bit of the world. The one thing you need to remember is that you'll be in boot camp with a whole lot of horny guys that are going to be away from their girl friends for the first time. There's going to be a lot of this…"

Joe reached out and grabbed Emmett's crotch. He didn't squeeze it, but he certainly held onto it for quite a few moments. Long enough to Emmett to start getting hard, despite the surprise of it.

This was all a bit too weird for Emmett. He wasn't particularly attracted to Joe, but he was still getting hard. Too long away from

Theison, he guessed. Joe just wasn't his type. He was in his early thirties, overweight and just not the personality that Emmett liked. But still, he was horny. Really, really horny. He just sat there and let the feelings flow.

"Yeah, they'll grab you and try to make you hard like this. Most of the time it'll be to make fun of you. But you'll need to watch out for the ones that want more than to embarrass you."

"Like you?" asked Emmett.

Joe paused and considered what he was doing. He really hadn't intended to assault this boy. But damn, he was gorgeous. At least he was as far as Joe was concerned. He'd admired Emmett's body all the time he'd worked for the bus company.

"Yeah, like me, I suppose." Joe released his hold and stepped away. "God, I'm sorry, Emmett. I really didn't mean to do that."

Emmett considered what'd just happened. He should be really pissed off by it. Really, really pissed. But then again, he could understand, in a deep recess of his mind, how it might happen. He knew that he wasn't completely masculine. He'd been told on more than one occasion that he came off as just a bit girlish at times. So, suppose Joe was gay. He'd have picked up on that and been fantasizing about it all this time. A situation then presented itself and he'd taken advantage of it to get a feel of the young guy.

"All right, Joe. I gather you find me attractive," Emmett said. Joe nodded, suddenly taken by surprise. This was not the reaction he'd expected. "I have to be honest, Joe, I'm not really attracted to you. But God help me, I'm horny as hell these days. My lover just moved to Montana and I haven't had any sex in the last month."

Hell, was he really about to suggest what he thought he was going to suggest? Emmett had never had sex with anyone that he hadn't been attracted to before. Why was he willing to now? Well, that was simple; he was horny and wanted some help getting off.

"I know you're expecting me to run out of here, Joe. I admit, that thought has crossed my mind. But quite frankly, I really want someone to get me off. So, if you really want to do this, I'll agree. But only this one time."

Joe simply nodded. He couldn't believe it. This beautiful teenager was going to let Joe give him a blow job. At least that's what he hoped he was being offered the chance at.

"But I am not going to sit here on this stool while you do it. I'm at least going to be comfortable."

Joe knew that he was being granted something special. It might have been nice for something mutual, but he supposed he couldn't really blame the boy. He'd come on too hard and too fast. Of course, that was understandable, since he'd never intended anything of the sort when he'd invited Emmett over. He'd simply taken a chance. Jesus, what had he been thinking? His bosses would have skinned him if he'd fucked this up, especially after the way he'd built up the boy in front of them.

They moved to the big lounge chair in the living room. Emmett wasn't in any mood for any foreplay or romanticism, so before he sat down, he undid his pants and pushed them and his underwear to the floor, then sat down and spread his legs.

Joe knew this was the only chance he'd ever get to taste this boy. He also knew, somehow, that if he said a word the chance would be taken away from him. He did the only thing he could; he knelt between those lightly haired legs and took Emmett's cock into his mouth, completely down his throat.

Emmett was a bit surprised that Joe had taken the whole thing right away, but he wasn't going to complain. For despite how this had all come about, it still felt mighty good. Joe really did know what he was about and he had Emmett at the cusp in no time. It didn't last more than five minutes, but it was a superior release and Emmett felt infinitely better for it. His jack off sessions just never seemed to empty him all the way.

Joe got up and brought him a damp cloth to wash himself with, and he was just fastening his pants when the doorbell rang. Ah, the pizza. That would go down a treat. They were into their second slice before either of them spoke.

"So, is this crisis really genuine or was this just a way to get me alone?"

Joe melted at this. "Gods Emmett, I never intended any of this. Yes, the problem is genuine and so is the pay. Please, I'm sorry. I enjoyed it, but I'm sorry all the same."

"All right, fair enough. I'll do the job. I'll start tomorrow night. I think it'd be best if I made my reports at the barn, though." The barn is what they called the yard where all the buses were stored and where the dispatch office was.

"That'd be great, Emmett."

They finished their pizza in silence and then Joe drove Emmett back to the bowling alley.

"Look, Joe," said Emmett before he stepped out of the car. "I'm not mad, all right? I'm just not attracted to you that way. We can still be friends, but I'd like to keep it as friends at work only, okay?"

"Yes, Emmett, that'd be just great."

With that Emmett went inside and picked up where he'd left off. Despite what had ultimately happened, he was thrilled with the prospect of making the extra money. Field trip pay would mean he'd be making twenty dollars an hour for sitting on his ass and riding a bus. How cool was that? He still had some of his school clothes that he'd stopped wearing because they were the wrong things to wear in his new role as an adult. But they would be perfect for this little job. He'd definitely come off as a high schooler.

Unfortunately for Emmett, the driver of the shuttle wasn't the least bit subtle or hesitant. He'd grown over-confident in his successes and hadn't considered the possibility of getting caught. The first night had been all that was necessary. He'd gotten on and off at several of the stops where he could see teens congregating. It was as he got on the third time that he picked up the telltale aroma of weed. The guy actually reeked of the stuff. And if that hadn't been enough, he'd actually offered to sell Emmett a joint.

Fortunately, Fridays was Emmett's usual day off at the alley, so he drove to the barn about ten. He'd decided that the best way to handle the events of Wednesday was simply to ignore that they'd ever happened. So when he arrived he was his usual jovial self.

"Hey ya, Joe. Got a trip ticket you need a driver for?"

That took Joe by surprise, but he recovered quickly, realizing what Emmett was saying about Wednesday. "Not right now, you greedy Gus. I always give you the plum runs anyway and now you want the cream too."

This had been their standard banter during the school year, so it let Joe know that things would be business as usual.

"So, you want my report, or have you got someone higher up that needs to hear it from the horses mouth?"

Joe frowned. "Damn, that can only be bad if you've got something already. Shit, I hate having to can him. Oh well, he brought it on himself. Let's go upstairs, the owner happens to be in today. He'll want to hear whatever you have to say for himself."

The owner was not the least bit pleased about the report. The liability issues were huge for them. He was, however, very pleased with the messenger. He immediately pulled out the business check register and wrote a two hundred dollar check right there on the spot and handed it to Emmett.

"Mr. Wingate, this is far more than I earned for the hours."

The owner smiled. "Not in my book, Mr. Page. You've saved this company from insurance issues and lawsuits from injuries as a result of an accident. Not to mention the legal ramifications should he have been stopped and arrested by the authorities while driving one of my buses."

He then turned to Joe. "Would you be terribly put out with me, Joe, if I offered the run to Mr. Page? I know he's only good for the summer, but he's certainly earned it in my book if he'd like the extra job."

"I don't have any complaints, Bill. He's always been one of my most reliable drivers."

"Well, Mr. Page, what do you think? Want to take the night shuttle for the summer? It'll give you a nice tidy little nest egg to take off to boot camp with you."

"That's very generous, Mr. Wingate. I'd be happy to take the run. I won't even have to give up my day job." They all laughed at that.

So for Emmett, it was a glorious summer. He worked his ass off; nine to five at the bowling alley and then six to midnight on the shuttle. His days off were different for each job so he ended up with four days a week with only one job; plenty of time to catch up on sleep. By the time September rolled around he had over five thousand dollars in the bank. Yes indeed, quite the tidy sum to begin a new life.

Boot camp hadn't been anywhere near the trouble Joe had alluded to. Sure there'd been grab assing in the showers, but no more than there'd ever been in the high school gym locker room. It was actually more enjoyable at boot camp. There wasn't nearly as much teenage hesitation. Oh, there was some; a few of the boys had lived a bit sheltered and were uncertain about many things. But overall, the majority of the guys were more assertive and more certain of themselves.

Boot camp was a time of being crammed into a small space; well, small for the eighty guys that comprise a company. There was no privacy what so ever. Your only alone time was in the bathroom stall. The 'head' stall; Emmett would have to get used to the term.

There was one bright moment for Emmett, and it had been totally unexpected and unplanned for. He'd been on Battalion watch one night. This meant that he roamed through the six company barracks and checked in with each of the company watch standers. It was no big thing. Simply a time for a short interaction with guys you normally only saw at a distance across the parade ground.

He made his patrol once every hour. He'd had a hard time locating one of the watches and had finally quietly stepped into the head as the location of last resort, expecting to find the watch relieving himself. Well, he'd found the watch relieving himself all right, but not in the way he'd expected. There he stood in a corner of the communal shower, his hand pumping for all it was worth. Emmett could only smile. The poor boy was so engrossed in what he was doing that he never heard Emmett walk up beside him.

"You having trouble getting that thing to fire?" Emmett had whispered.

The boy nearly killed himself when he spun around. He dropped his clipboard, but Emmett had been quick enough to catch it before it hit the floor. That would surely have awakened someone. What it accomplished, however, was to bring the boy's rock hard cock in front of Emmett's hungry mouth.

Even in the dim light of the head he could tell that the thing was beet red from being worked so hard. The boy was working furiously, trying to get it stuffed back into a place that was far too small to accommodate such an engorged instrument. The boy was also crying quietly, knowing that Emmett was going to make a scene.

Emmett's response was to take the boy's hands in his own and hold them still. "Shh. Don't sweat it, guy. I'm not going to rat on you."

That stopped the boy's crying and stilled his frantic efforts. "You're not?"

"Nah. We all gotta do it. But I have to say, you need to be gentler with it. You're going to hurt this thing you keep abusing it this bad."

"It's never taken this long to get off," he confessed after a moment's hesitation.

"Hey, sometimes Johnson has a mind of his own. How long you been working on this thing?"

"Ten fucking minutes. And look at it, it's harder than ever."

"So I see." Emmett looked up and saw that the boy was much more relaxed. He was one of the naive looking boys. He looked a bit younger than the required eighteen. But then, some boys simply didn't show their age as readily at this time of their lives. "You should try using lotion more often. Or at least some soap. Looks like it hurts right now."

"Gods, does it. But it just won't go down."

"Well, it's a fine looking cock. You need to take better care of it."

That statement got the boy's immediate attention. That is not the way most other guys would have put it. He sounded like Billy back home. He'd said the same thing many times when they were getting each other off.

Emmett recognized that look. It was one of knowledge and longing. This boy was not unused to getting a bit of help from time to time. "Tell you what, if you can keep a secret, I'll give you a hand this once."

"You won't tell anyone?"

"Hardly. I'm the one down here on the business end of this thing. I'm not likely to tell anyone and get my ass kicked out."

The boy simply nodded. So Emmett did just a bit more than 'give him a hand'. Another hand beating away at that thing would just have made matters worse anyway. So he used the only lubrication readily available. He swallowed that fine specimen and slowly blew the boy to release. It hadn't taken long, as Emmett had expected. It had been a fine orgasm, too; lots of the pearly white essence to satisfy him and lubricate his dry throat. He continued to gently suck on it until it went completely soft, and then he gently stuffed it back inside the boy's boxers and zipped up his pants.

When he stood, the boy was smiling big. "Gods, thanks a lot. That's better than Billy ever did."

Emmett simply squeezed the boy's shoulder. "You're welcome. Now, I need you to initial my round." And that was all there was to it; a bit of fun for Emmett, a little relief for the boy and then back to business as usual.

As Emmett completed his rounds and made his way back to the Battalion office, he realized that this was probably going to be what most of his sex life consisted of during his six year tour; the occasional blow job for a poor unfortunate that just needed a little help and encouragement. It wasn't likely that he'd ever encounter someone willing to make any sort of commitment. Well, if he resigned himself to the fact, he wouldn't be disappointed. This was supposed to be a time for getting a free education anyway; something that would carry him into a civilian career afterwards.

One of the perks of having been accepted into the nuclear power program was that the initial advancements were spectacularly quick and automatic at the end of each of his three training phases, so long as the candidate passed each phase. The first of these quick promotions came just before the final graduation ceremonies in boot camp.

Most of the recruits left for their first schools as an E-1 with a single diagonal slash on their rank/rate insignia. That designated them as a seaman recruit. But Emmett would leave with three of those stripes. He'd be an E-3, or seaman. That meant a significant difference in his monthly pay. Instead of the fourteen hundred dollar monthly rate of the new E-1, he would be receiving sixteen hundred and fifty dollars each month. Not bad pay for someone for whom housing and food were provided for. Even his initial stock of working clothes were provided for at no cost. And then, of course there was the free medical care.

Emmett's only recurring personal bill for several years was the cell phone service he signed up for right after graduation from boot camp. His one major purchase after graduation was a brand new, top of the line laptop computer.

His Navy life went on uneventfully for several months after boot camp. He finished a short six week school in San Diego before moving on to the promised Advanced Electronics School in Great Lakes, Illinois. The base was located north of Chicago. It was a large training facility with all manner of disciplines being educated to supply new, well trained sailors for the fleet. Being a well established training base, there was ample barracks space. But Emmett and a fellow sailor wanted something more private, so they found an apartment off base where they could get away from the hustle of the hurry up routine that was typical of the base.

He made several friends over the first month. One in particular really caught his interest. Not because he was overly cute, but simply because he seemed so introverted and lonely. He was a smart kid, really. He certainly had a better handle on the electronics theories that Emmett was struggling with. So he'd befriended Mark by the simple expedient of asking for his help with the homework. Mark was just barely eighteen and seemed flattered that this now twenty year old would take an interest and a liking to him. His mind was still wrapped around the high school philosophy that one year in age meant a world of difference.

Emmett did his best to teach him otherwise. The tutoring helped Mark to see that age really wasn't all that important. Their two year difference didn't mean that Emmett knew it all. Mark was a great tutor too. He could take the incomprehensible theories and explain them in plain terms that the instructors never used. Emmett's grades quickly improved significantly and he was always quick to give the praise to his tutor.

The one thing that Mark seemed to have a problem with was a very over powering body odor. It was several weeks before Emmett was able to find out the reason. He'd gone looking for Mark one Saturday in the early afternoon. This was a time when the barracks was pretty deserted because everyone was out cutting loose after a week of hard schooling. It took Emmett quite a while to locate Mark, and he'd finally found the boy in the shower. What he saw when he came around the corner into the communal shower was Mark, all by himself, and there wasn't a hair on his body. Nothing, nowhere. Well, almost nowhere. Mark was close enough to the entrance and his hair was pitch black, so it was easy to see a few stray hairs at the base of Marks fully, man sized cock.

Some things immediately fell into place in Emmett's mind. Mark had immediately turned toward the wall to hide himself.

"Gees, Mark, I've been looking all over for you. I thought I'd take you out and buy you lunch to say thanks for all your help."

"Uh, yeah, sure, that'd be great." But he didn't turn around. So Emmett decided to take a direct approach to the problem. He stepped into the shower and gently laid his hands on Mark's shoulders. Mark immediately stiffened up.

"Hey, buddy," said Emmett, "relax, I'm not going to hurt you." He forced Mark to turn around. "Is this the only time you can get a shower without being harassed?"

Mark's eyes flew open. This was not any sort of reaction he'd gotten before. Emmett wasn't teasing him. He looked, in fact, quite concerned. Mark simply nodded.

"Fuckers. So, you just a late bloomer?"

"No," he answered hesitantly. "The doctors have all said I have a rare condition that prevents body hair from growing like most guys get."

"Wow. Never heard of anything like that. You ever going to be normal?"

"Oh yeah, they said it'll just take me a lot longer."

"Well, we can't have you going all week without a shower, Mark. Tell you what, I'll stick around after classes and I'll come shower with you. We'll see if we can't get the guys to give you a break."

"Really?"

"Yeah, really. It's not good for you to have to go without a shower like this. I bet you get ribbed about your odor, don't you?"

"Yeah, but it's better than the crap Barry throws at me in here."

"Ah, big tough, macho, Barry. Yeah, he can be a real asshole. Well, we'll nip that one soon enough. Now, why don't you finish up and we'll go have that lunch."

Mark was all smiles and enthusiasm the rest of the weekend. He couldn't believe that someone had finally accepted him. Someone that didn't make fun of him; who'd even offered to help with the abuse. Though he didn't know what that help would be, he felt like a regular guy with Emmett. Mark's hairlessness was not an issue for his friend.

Monday afternoon arrived all too soon, however, and Mark was not looking forward to the shower. But he'd promised Emmett that he'd be there. The place was crowded as always. Everyone seemed to need a shower before they could head off for the chow hall. He felt immediately better, though, when he entered and saw Emmett already under a spray about halfway down the room.

It took all his courage to walk the length of the room to reach the only unused shower head. And as luck would have it, Barry was directly across the room from him.

"Hey, look, our little girlie has shown up!"

There were a few weak chuckles around the room, but no one seemed to be terribly enthusiastic about the subject. As Emmett had suggested, Mark simply ignored the remark and proceeded with his shower.

"Hey, come on girlie, let's see that baby body."

"You guys ever notice how it always seems to be the pin pricks that are the loudest?" said Emmett. The room got instantly silent.

"Who you calling a pin prick, ass hole?"

"See, he even knows who I'm talking about."

When Barry rushed up to him, Emmett didn't even hesitate. He pulled back and slugged Barry right in the gut, lifting him a foot off the floor. Well, the guy hadn't been expecting it and he immediately fell to his knees, trying to get his wind back.

"You guys ever hear about Orinet's Syndrome?" There were heads shaking all over the room. "Well, it's a very rare medical condition that prevents hair from growing like it does for most of us. Anyone that has it could be twenty-five or thirty before he has what we all take for granted." Emmett grabbed Barry's hair and pulled it back hard, forcing the bully to look at him. "So I'll make this simple for you, Barry. I hear one word of you harassing someone who can't help it that his body isn't normal and I'll rip your fucking heart out and feed it to you while you watch. You got it?!" Barry simply nodded, he still couldn't speak. "Good. Now I think your shower is done for the day. Get your fucking ass out of my sight before you really piss me off."

There was never another word spoken on the subject. Mark was able to shower normally without the abuse. Sure, the guys would look, it was only natural, but Mark didn't mind the looking. He knew he was a strange sight. But the guys were friendly after that.

"What's Orinet's Syndrome?" asked Mark when they returned to his room. "The doctors always said that my condition had never been given a name."

"Haven't a clue, Mark. I made it up on the spot. Sounded impressive, did it?"

Mark laughed.

The up side of it was that Barry seemed to have taken the incident as a sign from God that he'd better straighten himself out.

He even apologized to Mark a few weeks later, right in the shower, in front of everyone present.

Well, Emmett became Mark's hero after that and they became even closer. He would usually spend the weekends at Emmett's apartment off base. He soon learned that he could talk to Emmett about anything. No subject was taboo. Not even sex.

And that is how it all began for them one night at the apartment.

"What's it like?" asked Mark out of the blue.

"I'll be happy to explain," Emmett laughed, "as soon as you define what 'it' is."

"Oh sorry, I was thinking about sex."

Emmett got very quiet for a moment. This could be dangerous ground where their friendship was concerned. Mark was cute enough, after all, and Emmett had seen all the usual fascinating parts and liked what he saw. But he didn't want to say anything here that would drive Mark away. The friendship was very important to him.

"Well Mark, that's all pretty personal."

"Oh, I'm sorry. We don't have to talk about it."

"No, Mark, you misunderstand what I'm saying. Each person's experience in life and the way their bodies are wired together give each person a slightly different experience. The simple answer is that sex is probably the greatest shared activity I know of. Two people melding their bodies together and exploring each other fully can be the best high ever created. And it has the advantage of being totally legal and natural.

"Now unfortunately, I can only really give you information from one perspective. There's sex with women and then there's sex with...."

"Men," Mark provided. He sat there for several moments without saying a word. "You probably can't help me then. You'll only know about girls."

Emmett smiled at his friend, and this surprised Mark. He'd known Emmett wouldn't kick him out. That wasn't his style. He was the most accepting guy Mark had ever met. He never judged a person. He never forced his ideas on you. He gave you the best information he had or directed you to where you could get that information. But still, admitting he was interested in having sex with guys would bring a certain level of distaste. But no, Emmett simply smiled.

"I gather by the shocked look that you never guessed," Emmett said.

"You mean… You mean you… You're… gay?"

"Well, you have to admit that it's not something that a guy in the Navy would be real thrilled about having as public knowledge. It tends to end military careers."

"Is it as great as I've always dreamed it is?"

"Well now, Mark, that depends on who you're with and what their aspirations are. If all your partner is looking for is his own pleasure, then no, it's not all that fantastic. You'll walk away from the experience unfulfilled and feeling pretty crummy about yourself."

"But what if it's with someone you really like, and who likes you?" Mark asked shyly.

"Well, then it can be the most intense experience of your life. The key is to be with someone that is more interested in making sure you enjoy yourself than in getting the enjoyment. That's always when it works the best."

Emmett went on to give the boy the examples from his own experiences. He started with how unfulfilled he felt after the Joe incident. But then he went on to describe what he and Theison had shared. "So all that means is that you'll have some good sexual experiences, some pretty crummy ones, and then you'll occasionally have the kind that rocks your world."

"You know so much," sighed Mark.

"I have to admit that I think I'm one of the lucky ones, Mark. I was always able to keep that side of my life a secret and still managed to meet other like-minded guys. It's pretty unusual really. I've known a lot of guys that didn't have it so easy."

Mark looked longingly at him, and there was no doubt what thought was coursing through that sex starved, virgin boy.

"Come over here, Mark."

When Mark moved to sit next to him, Emmett intercepted the move and summarily planted the boy on his lap and simply cuddled and held him. Mark was more than willing to participate. He wrapped his arms around Emmett's shoulders and laid his head on his own arm. He sighed in real contentment.

"You're absolutely certain that you'd like to try this, Mark?"

"I've wanted to try this forever. But I don't have much of a bod..."

Emmett put the fingers of one hand over Mark's mouth. "I don't want to hear any of that, Mark. You have a perfectly fine body. You're not fat, you have all the requisite parts, and they are very good looking parts I might add. And you're a genuinely fun person to be with. And now I find that you're a great hugger."

That got a chuckle out of Mark.

"I'm absolutely thrilled to be here with you, Mark. I admit that I've never thought of you in these terms, but mainly because I've really cherished our friendship and I wasn't going to allow a bit of lust on my part to interfere. But if this is truly something you want to experience with me then I am honored to be your first and more than willing to accommodate you."

Emmett lifted Mark's face so that they were looking eye to eye. He then leaned slowly forward. Mark never pulled away. He never hesitated. When their lips met he returned as good as he got. Well, for a boy with no professed experience, he was beginning rather well. There was eagerness in this kiss as evidenced by the slight trembling from this small body. But there was also technique, surprisingly.

Emmett began slowly. No need scaring this boy by trying to dive down his throat. This was intended to be a get acquainted kiss. But Mark had other ideas. It was he that initiated the first move with his tongue. He hesitantly began licking at Emmett's lips gently and slowly. It would have been so easy to simply open up and pull him fully inside, but Emmett knew this boy well enough now to know that aggression would scare him away.

The poor kid was frightened of everything and everyone. He'd been so picked on all his life that he'd never had the chance to develop any self confidence, no assertiveness. So Emmett had been working slowly to build just those qualities. Always allowing Mark to lead, letting him make decisions that concerned them both. Little things mostly; where to go, what to do. But it was having the desired effect. The more he came to realize that he could, in fact, make decisions and that nothing bad would come of them, he'd begun to assert himself just a bit more everyday.

This act of losing his virginity was the biggest decision making opportunity of his young life, and Emmett was determined to let Mark be the lead in this experience. He was confident that when Mark came to a point where he was unsure of the direction they should go that he would ask. Emmett had managed to instill that much into the boy by this time. He knew for a certainty that he could ask anything of Emmett and the older boy would never make fun of him but would take the time to answer as fully as he was capable of. Emmett was the ultimate…and the best…mentor.

When Mark made a tentative stab at Emmett's lips, he slowly opened them and allowed Mark to enter his body. It was a symbolic gesture yet so important. It was his very first experience at having any part of himself inside another person. And as their tongues met and caressed for the first time, Mark moaned.

Emmett cracked an eye open and was touched by the few tears he saw on Mark's face. This was his first experience at two souls touching and he was being moved by it. He was allowing his emotions to be free, something Mark had trouble in doing. He was a sensitive boy and had always been ridiculed because of the unmanly behavior.

They kissed for quite some time, fully exploring the others' mouth. They were also doing a bit of tentative exploring of each others' bodies. Mark had begun by simply embracing a bit more firmly, but soon he inched his hands up until he was caressing Emmett's hair. When that seemed to go well, he began to move his other hand down and began rubbing Emmett's back, gently at first, but as the kiss progressed his touch became firmer, and yes, lustful.

When Mark finally pulled away and stared into Emmett's eyes, he was thrilled. He'd done it! He'd kissed a boy!! And he'd loved it!!!

Emmett smiled and leaned forward and gently kissed away the tears from Mark's face. "That is so sweet, baby."

'He called me baby! Yeah!' thought Mark.

"That was incredible, Babe. You sure you've never done this before?" Emmett felt that he needed to lighten it up just a touch so that Mark could relax into this experience.

"That was awesome, Em," he whispered, tentatively trying for some little pet name that this glorious man would accept from him. And then Mark blushed as he became aware of his own body's reaction to this. "Em, I'm hurting a bit."

Emmett smiled, knowing precisely what Mark's problem was. "Stand up, babe, and we'll relieve a bit of that pressure." When he stood, Emmett was not surprised by the bulge he saw. He 'was' a bit surprised by the telltale wet spot that had soaked through his underwear and then through the thick material the Navy used for their trousers. "My god, babe, you're going to pop the zipper if we don't get you out of them."

He'd intended to start at the top and work his way down Mark's body, but changed his mind when he realized that the boy probably 'was' in considerable discomfort. Mark tended to wear briefs that were too small for his package, so this over hard cock of his would be straining big time. So Emmett simply and efficiently undid the buckle, button and zipper and pulled down his trousers and briefs to the middle of Mark's thighs; just enough to allow his engorged member to be free. And man, was it ever hard. Mark's cock was obviously straining. The deep red of that normally pale organ and the pulsing bounce to the beat of Mark's rapidly beating heart gave ample evidence of this boy's full acceptance of this event. The head glistened with the moisture of his precum as it continued to flow. It didn't drip, it flowed, ribbons of it oozing down toward the floor.

"Em, I don't think I can hold it any longer," Mark begged. "I'm too close!"

Well that was not an unexpected reaction. So Emmett simply reached up and gently caressed Mark's cock a couple of times, knowing full well that this would be a spectacular event, and one he wanted to watch, despite his great desire to taste Mark's essence. Three full strokes was all it took and Mark was shooting his brains out. They were only a foot apart, so Mark's release easily covered the distance and splashed onto Emmett's face, and then his chin. The remainder shot just far enough to break free of the glans and then fell to his lap and the floor.

"Ahh! Ahh! Ooh! Eeeehhhhh!"

Oh that was a glorious sound. Emmett hated quiet cummers. He loved nothing more than to hear his partner's enjoyment. A vocal orgasm was always more intense, because it forced the entire body to relax and thoroughly participate.

When he'd spent his last, Mark's hands grasped Emmett's shoulders for support as his knees shook from the experience. He'd never felt like that before. His whole body tingled like it'd never done before. It was the orgasm of his life!

Emmett took the opportunity to gently pull Mark toward him and he slowly milked that eight inch, narrow weapon to get the last drops. They tasted just as sweet as he thought they might. He carefully cleaned every inch, trying not to touch the over sensitive head too much. He really didn't want Mark pulling out. This was one sweet cock. How could this boy's cock taste and feel so…young? But it was true. There was a quality to this organ that screamed its inexperience.

"Oh, Em, please, I can't stand anymore."

So Emmett helped him fall gently to his knees and then he pulled Mark to him and hugged him to his chest. He caressed Mark's back, his head, ran his fingers through the thin dark black hair. He waited. He basked in the heat of this young body in his arms. He relished each heave of Mark's shoulders as he frantically tried to replenish his depleted oxygen levels. He thoroughly enjoyed the afterglow of Mark's first experience.

As his breathing began to return to something resembling normal, Mark was able to better take in his surroundings. The first thing that finally penetrated his mind was how absolutely glorious it felt to be held in this man's embrace. It was a magnificent place he found himself in. Accepted…and yes…even loved. There'd been far too little of that in his life.

His parents had raised him well, but they were not overly affectionate. They loved him, he knew that, but as he'd gotten older, they'd stepped down the demonstrations of affection. Some misguided belief that it wasn't manly, or something of the sort, he assumed. Or maybe, just maybe, they'd seen something of his desires in his eyes and were uncomfortable in encouraging him to express those desires, especially with them.

It was all too much to think about. All that mattered was this moment, this man, this glory.

He was in such a position that when he opened his eyes finally, the first thing he saw was the puddle of cum in Emmett's lap. It looked decidedly odd sitting there; his cum, his bodily fluids sitting in the lap of another person. And then a thought occurred to him. What would it be like to watch a guy cum? What does it feel like to hold another man's cock in your hand? What did it taste like?

Well, those questions just had to be answered. And the bulge beneath that puddle of cum just screamed to Mark. He reached down and began gently running one finger through the puddle of goo, feeling the hardness of Emmett's body beneath. At the first touch, that marvelous bulge jumped. It strained the material of Em's pants as if begging to be released.

Mark reached behind Em and pulled his butt toward the front of the chair, until his cheeks were just at the edge, then he reached up and began removing the obstacles to the glories hidden within. He was gentle, but he was not hesitant. It took no time, really, until he was pulling trousers and boxer briefs down and off Em's legs, pulling the shoes off as he did so.

And there it was; a man sized erect cock and large balls. He simply sat there for a few moments and took in the sight. His wildest dreams had never conjured anything close to this sight. It stood at full mast, bouncing slightly. The balls moved within their fleshy sack, as if saying, see me, see me, I'm full. And the heat. Gods, the heat was incredible. Never had he imagined that there'd be such a wave of intense desire being transmitted to him through the simple expedient of temperature.

He put his hands on Em's knees and slowly crept towards his objective. The hair beneath his hands was soft and slightly damp. The muscles were quivering. So many things about this moment simply radiated desire, longing. This was so much more than Mark had ever imagined it would be. It wasn't just about getting a release. There were experiences to enjoy that had nothing to do with release, but had everything to do with desire and passion. They made the experience so much greater.

Finally, he was there. A mere centimeter separated him from a penis and testicles that were not his own. The most intimate, private area of another man's body stood open to him. His left hand dipped down and cupped those sensitive orbs. He could feel their life, the hair gently tickling the palm of his hand. He caressed them and rolled them softly. Em moaned. It was a remarkable experience to elicit this enjoyment in another guy.

And finally, the moment of truth. The moment of years of fantasies was before him. His right hand gently wrapped itself around another man's throbbing, pulsing manhood.

"Oooh," they sighed in unison.

It was hard, and yet it was soft as well. It seemed to be just a bit longer than his own, but it was definitely thicker. The head was very wet from the precum and Mark never hesitated. He leaned forward and licked that moisture into his mouth and tasted, for the first time, something of this man's essence. Certainly not the full taste of cum, but still, it was fluid that had been generated by another. Oh, and it was good. He hadn't known what to expect, precisely. Sure, he'd tasted himself from time to time, but this was so much more. This was the excitement of savoring another man's body. There was also just a touch of shame. But that small touch was far overshadowed by the excitement.

Society said this was wrong. Two men should never want to be this intimate, this familiar with each other. But want it he did.

It was now an overpowering desire. He wanted this more than he'd wanted anything in his life. Fuck society, fuck consequences. This is who he was, there was no doubt in his mind. When love mattered, this is where he had to be.

He smiled as he finally understood himself. This moment was an epiphany. HE…WAS…GAY! It had a glorious sound as it echoed in his mind. This was right! That little taste of shame shattered beneath the onslaught of that revelation. 'Fuck you, world! This is who I am and I love it!'

It was so over powering. He leaned in and swallowed Em's cock. Took nearly all of it before he felt himself begin to gag.

"Easy, Mark, don't force it," said Em softly. There was a far away quality to his voice. "You're doing incredible. Don't take any more than you can this time."

So Mark accepted the guidance and simply nodded up and down on that magnificent cock. His left hand continued to massage Em's balls. He let his right hand slip down until it was nestled in that remarkable mass of hair at the base. Up and down. The hair was so soft. Up and down. Em's nuts began to contract up into his crotch. Up and down. The taste of the increased flow of precum was glorious. Up and down. The nuts stopped moving, the head inside his mouth grew to new sizes, the cock got incredibly hard. Up and down.

"Oooooohhhhhhhh!"

Mark purposely took the first volley into his mouth and then he pulled off and began stroking that pulsing organ to release the rest of the offering. He ran his first taste of cum around in his mouth as he marveled at the sight of cum spurting over and over again from the bright red glans. It was a remarkable sensation, feeling that silky, slightly salty juice coating his tongue. And then he swallowed. 'Oooh, yes,' he thought. 'This is the stuff of gods.'

He stroked Em's cock until nothing seemed left, then, just as Em had done, he leaned in and took that cock back into his mouth and performed the same cleaning ritual. When he was sure he'd gotten all there was to give, he pulled off and licked his own hand clean, always savoring, always wanting just a bit more of this man's liquor. Yes! That was what it was. It had to be, because Mark was high from consuming it.

When he looked up, it was into the glassy eyed, smiling face of...Em. This was the full man. There was nothing being held back, nothing being hidden. This was everything that he was. All his barriers and protections were down and Mark was awed by what he sensed. There was such passion and love in this man. It wasn't all sexual. It was a part of everything he was and did. But he couldn't let much of it be seen in the normal day to day world, because that would have let out the sensual and sexual parts as well, and that was a danger.

Mark got up from the floor and pushed Em's legs together and then sat on them. They kissed, long and slow. Then they simply laid their heads on each other's shoulders as they basked in this moment of supreme sharing.

"That was awesome, baby."

"Yes, it was."

"How would you feel about a shower? One like we could never take at the barracks?"

Mark could only nod. This was going to be a glorious night. For, though he knew in his heart that he wanted to try this, he'd been more than just a bit frightened at the prospect; all those years of doubt, all those lectures from various people about the evils of homosexuality. Hearing all the horror stories of guys begin beaten and abused because of their choice of intimate partners. They all led to some serious questions about the wisdom of his desires.

But that was all gone now. Fuck em. This was heaven. This was glory. This was true intimacy. THIS was who he was.

They stripped the remainder of their clothes right there in the living room. Emmett only paused as they entered the bathroom to wash the cum from his trousers. While he did this, Mark went to the antique claw foot tub and set the temperature of the water and pulled the shower curtain all around the thing. Then and only then did he switch the outlet to the shower head.

They stepped in one after the other and ensured the curtain was properly positioned; neither wanted to have to mop up the floor.

Then they turned and gently embraced and kissed, briefly. Mark took the lead by grabbing the soap first and began washing Emmett.

It was a marvelous experience washing another body. He worked slowly from top to bottom. He washed Emmett's upper half and then skipped down to his legs. When it came time to hit all the more interesting areas, he gave his crotch a quick, yet thorough wash, and then he stepped up and hugged Emmett. Then he began washing Emmett's lower back, slowly working his way down until he was washing his firm round buns. And then came his moment of truth. Mark placed his middle finger at the crest of the channel that led to regions he'd wondered if he'd be able to go. But he started his hand in motion and didn't stop until he couldn't reach under Emmett any further.

The only part of the experience that surprised him was Emmett's reaction. As Mark's finger passed over his asshole, he leaned slightly back, pushing himself into the finger. And he'd shuddered and moaned in delight. Gees, could it really feel that good having someone touching you there?

"Is it really that good?"

"Oh, baby, it's an incredible feeling." He pushed Mark away. "Here, let me have my turn, and if you're game I'll show you."

"Ok, you've got me interested now. I mean it never really feels all that great when I do it to myself."

Emmett simply smiled and began the same routine as Mark had used. When the moment finally arrived, Emmett hugged him, face to face, and began the exact same process, so Mark was fully aware of when the moment had arrived. He forced himself to relax as he felt Emmett's finger begin to travel down his chute. And then the most incredible thing in the world happened; Emmett's finger made contact with his sphincter and it was like someone had stuck an electric probe against his ass.

"Hhhiiiiiiissssssss!" he breathed as his automatic reaction was to push back into that glorious probe.

Well, there was no doubt as to his enjoyment. Emmett could feel this body vibrating as it pushed harder and harder against his probing finger.

"Put it in, Em, please, put it in," begged Mark.

So Emmett did it. He could feel the openness of that marvelous bud, so he pushed slightly. Mark responded by pushing further back. His finger slipped inside without any effort. Gods, was this boy hot for this. In moments Mark was moving back and forth while Emmett simply held his finger steady.

"Oh god. Oh shit. Oh hell."

The next thing he knows, Emmett feels Mark swallow his cock and begin sucking on it like a Hoover vacuum. He had to lean forward over Mark's head slightly to maintain his finger's position. Fortunately Emmett was a bit taller than Mark so it was just possible to attain that position and still have Mark jutting back and forth.

Emmett had a sudden idea and reached under Mark with his free hand and simply wrapped it around his hard cock. All Emmett had to do was hold on, Mark was doing all the work. The boy was so excited by all this that it only took a couple of minutes before his ass slammed shut around Emmett's finger and his cock let loose. That was all it took for Emmett, he unloaded into Mark's mouth. He had one brief thought as he let fly. 'Shit, I hope he doesn't choke.'

Their simultaneous orgasms were enormous despite their recent discharges. When all was said and done Mark knelt down and sat back on his legs, which was a good thing because Emmett needed to kneel before he fell. Then they collapsed into each others' arms and simply breathed.

When they were both breathing a bit more normally, Emmett made an observation.

"I believe this would be one of those world rocking times, baby."

"I know it is for me," breathed Mark as he sat up and looked into Emmett's eyes. "Em, this has been the best night of my life. Thank you so much."

Emmett reached up and caressed his face with one hand. "You're welcome, babe. And thank you. I haven't enjoyed myself this much since Theison left for Montana."

That brought out the sun. The smile had all the warmth and shine of that noon time presence.

They spent the last six weeks of school experimenting and experiencing, so that by the time they were given orders for separate parts of the world, Mark was as confident a man as anyone else at the school. He was no longer the retiring wall flower. He walked taller, spoke clearer and never allowed himself to become the butt of someone else's jest.

Their final night was a bit tearful, but not overly so. They'd spent many hours discussing the future and the fact that they had no choice but to become separated for the next five years. They agreed that they may never meet again, but if that were so, they had the memories of this time, and they were glorious memories to have.

Emmett was sent to Orlando, Florida for his next school. This was the big one; Nuclear Power School. It was here that he'd learn about nuclear fission. It was also going to be the biggest challenge of his life. He'd found the concepts of electricity confusing; how much more confusing would be this near magical process of nuclear fission and the controlling of the process. He went there with more than just a little trepidation.

The school was a new one. The old school had been located in the northern part of the country, but had been so old that the Navy decided to update the facility and move it to a warmer climate. So the school was brand new; not a year old. Correspondingly, the barracks for the students of this school were new as well. They were some of the best living quarters Emmett had yet encountered. The buildings were three stories tall and very long. They were broken into living pods. Each pod had a common room off of which were four rooms in which lived two students each.

The beds could be configured as bunks or taken apart so that both were on the floor, depending on the wishes of the occupants. Each room had its own bathroom and shower; a rarity in barracks design. Each room had two large cabinets where each man would hang his uniforms and civilian clothes, with two large drawers in the bottom for all their personal items. There was one shared desk and a small TV stand with cable hook up.

The occupants of each pod were even allowed to alter their own room assignments as personalities dictated; but only within each pod. It was the most amazing arrangement that any of them had encountered. The shuffling of sailors within the pod made it easy to configure themselves so that there was a minimum of personal conflicts.

Pod assignments were made so that only students in the same class lived in a pod. It took everyone a couple of weeks to really start to get to know their pod mates, but there was plenty of time. The school was a six month long affair and wasn't even slated to begin until two months after Emmett's arrival.

Emmett's room mate was Riley, who was a year younger. He was a good looking guy and had a bigger build than Emmett. There didn't appear to be any fat on him, he was just a larger guy. He was a few inches shorter than Emmett, but he held himself confidently. He had a generally powerful appearance. This completely contrasted to his quiet nature. Not introverted. Not naïve. Not the least bit unsure of himself. He was just soft spoken.

Riley was a very nice change from some of the other guys in the pod who were very boisterous. Emmett tended to fit in the middle of the two extremes. One thing that he really liked about Riley was his sense of humor. When in a social situation he tended to be quiet, and everyone thought he was shy. But Emmett soon learned that Riley was an observer. He saw *everything* that went on around him. After they'd go back to their room Riley would regale him with his humorous observations of the goings on they'd just left. He could have Emmett in stitches in minutes.

The very best thing about Riley, however, was his lack of modesty. He wasn't the least bit shy about having his body on display. If Emmett couldn't exercise his gay side openly, at least he had plenty of eye candy for his shower-time entertainments.

The two of them got along so well, in fact, that they were soon going out and doing things together away from the base. They both reasoned that seeing the sights was always more fun if you could do it with someone. Neither of them cared to go out with the raucous groups that seemed to be the norm around the barracks.

They went everywhere. They started, as did most everyone, at Disney World. That park alone took them five trips to see all they wanted to. There was, of course, Sea World, Circus World, and Universal Studios, too. Hell, the list just seemed to go on and on.

After three weeks, it seemed that they'd been everywhere and done everything. They were both exhausted from it all and decided to take a week off to recover. Since everyone else seemed to be inclined to continue the party, that left Riley and Emmett the only ones in their pod for that week.

Being an avid reader, Emmett had no trouble occupying his time and relaxing. Riley was more inclined to watch TV or lie on his bunk and simply listen to music with his headphones on.

On this particular day, Emmett had walked over to the base library to pick out a couple of new books. He'd planned to read at the library for a while, but after making his selections, he decided to go on back to the room and read in his bunk so that he could listen to music while he read.

When he entered the room, he got an unexpected surprise. Riley was laying on his bunk, his headphones on, stripped naked and was slowly jacking off with his eyes closed.

Well, Emmett could have handled that a couple of different ways. His first inclination was to simply sit on his bunk and watch the show, but reasoned that that approach would have ultimately alienated his room mate and he wasn't prepared to have to break in a new one. Besides, he really liked Riley. They seemed to be a perfect match.

So, Emmett closed the door and then reached out and grabbed one of Riley's big toes and shook it.

Well, Riley's eyes shot open and he blushed a deep red. The shade tended to clash with the dark brown hair on his head. But Emmett simply smiled as Riley pulled his headphones off with one hand and tried to cover his crotch with the other. That proved to be problematic since Riley was a well hung as Emmett and his hand just could not cover all the jewels.

"Oh hell, Emmett!"

"Don't sweat it, Riley. I just thought you'd like to know that you had an audience."

Riley got a slightly puzzled look on his face. That was an unusual way of responding to finding your room mate jacking off.

Emmett decided that the best way to handle the situation was to simply be casual about the whole thing. So he simply walked over and started fussing with his small stereo and putting his books on his headboard shelf. When he finally turned around and sat on his bunk, he found that Riley had slipped on a pair of boxers and was sitting on the edge of his bunk, simply looking at him.

"What?" asked Emmett.

"You're not pissed off?"

"Nah. Why should I be pissed off? We all do it."

"You gonna tell everyone?"

"Hell no!" Emmett sighed. "Look, Riley, I'm not offended, I'm not pissed off, and no one is ever going to hear about this." Emmett decided to take a bit of a chance and leaned back onto his elbows so that his bulging crotch was visible.

"Whoa!" breathed Riley.

"Ok, so now we both have a secret," said Emmett as he sat back up. "It's no one's business, Riley. I imagine there are a lot of circle jerks going on all over the base. This is an organization that promotes that sort of thing. They stuff all these horny young guys together and there just are not enough females to go around."

Riley simply sat there for the longest time, simply staring at Emmett. This was a situation that thrilled him. But that could get him into so much trouble. He liked the Navy and he didn't want to get booted out, but he really found Emmett sexy. These past three weeks had been a real treat for him. It'd been like one long date with one of the best looking guys he could imagine. Every jack off session he'd had since arriving here had been about Emmett.

Emmett finally got up. "I'll just go take a bit of a walk and let you finish up, if you'd like."

"Uh...you don't have to," said Riley, hesitantly.

Ok, this was getting neither of them anywhere. Emmett had seen something in Riley's eyes. There'd been interest and perhaps a bit of longing.

"Ok, I'll stay. But if I stay, I'm going to watch."

Riley smiled.

"Or, if you'd rather, I'll help." There it was. He'd stuck his dick out there and now he'd find out if Riley was going to stomp on it.

Riley really smiled this time. "Only if I get to help you with your problem."

Emmett's answer was to simply start to undress. It wasn't a sexy thing, but he didn't rush through the process either. When he was finally down to just his boxer briefs he stopped and really looked at Riley. He was riveted. So Emmett stepped over and simply caressed his cheek. Riley leaned into the caress and closed his eyes.

Oh hell, that felt so fabulous. Emmett had such soft hands, and he was so gentle. He stood up and opened his eyes and looked into Emmett's and then he leaned in and kissed him. He felt the hand on his cheek move to the back of his head and pull him in tightly as the other hand came around him and pulled him fully into Emmett.

Emmett had to lean his head down just a bit, but not enough to force the rest of their bodies to move apart. Feeling their mutual erections pressed against one another was awesome. He pressed his advantage and opened his mouth.

When he felt Emmett's mouth open, Riley immediately took full advantage. He opened up and stabbed into that hot orifice and began to do battle with what he found there. They both gave up completely and let their combined passions take over. But although their tongues fought for supremacy, their hands remained gentle and loving as they explored each others' back, head and butt. Their crotches ground together tightly and they soon reached a point where neither of them could hold out and they came at almost the same instant onto their stomachs; for though they hadn't realized it, their cocks had become so hard that they were now poking out of the tops of their underwear. They clung to each other tightly as they came, moaning into each others' mouth, their tongues motionless as their cocks pulsed out their pent up longing.

When the worst was over they disengaged their mouths so that they could breathe. But they never relinquished their hold on one another, clinging for the support that the other provided. It took several minutes before they could speak.

"Wow, that was awesome," said Riley softly.

"Yes it was. So now, I just have to know, Riley, are you gay or just willing to have some fun?"

Riley pulled back and looked at him. "No, I'm gay. That going to be a problem?"

Emmett smiled. "Hardly. Well, I guess it will, a bit. How are we ever going to manage to keep our hands off each other?"

Riley laughed. "That *will* be a problem."

They both laughed.

"Ok," said Emmett, "You're first in the shower." There was, after all, not enough room for two in it. As Riley stepped by him, he reached out and swatted Riley's ass. "I've been wanting to do that for weeks."

Riley continued on but looked over his shoulder, "And I've been wanting you to."

Emmett pulled out a clean wash cloth from his locker and walked into the bathroom and up to the sink. No sense letting their cum dry before he got his chance at the shower. He then walked over and pulled back the curtain and stuck his head into the shower. "No fair playing with it, either." Then he leaned forward and gave the occupant a quick kiss.

By the time he finished pissing, something that he always seemed to have to do after cumming, Riley was done and stepping out of the still running shower.

"Next," said Riley as he watched Emmett shake off the last few drops. As Emmett approached to get into the shower Riley grabbed him and kissed him. "How'd we get so lucky?"

"Ah, the gods have always favored me," answered Emmett with a laugh as he stepped into the shower.

It wasn't long before they were back in the main room, laying on Emmett's bunk. The advantage of Navy bunks is that they were all twin size and that forced them to have to lay on their sides and very, very close. At least that was their excuse.

"So, Riley, have you always known you were gay?"

"Always is a long time, Emmett. But I've known since I was thirteen. I started with my older brother, he was fifteen. It was just fun for him, but I knew immediately that it was all I ever wanted."

"It was the next door neighbor's kid for me. We were twelve. Then there was the senior from the high school who assisted my track coach when I was fourteen. That's when I really knew."

"This is great, Emmett. I'm starting to look forward to this school after all."

"Yeah, me too. I'm looking forward to enjoying myself, now. Not going to be so easy once we get stationed onboard ship."

"That's the truth," sighed Riley. "Oh well, we knew what we were letting ourselves in for when we enlisted."

"Yes we did. But it's still a shame."

"At least it'll be easy for the next seven months. Being room mates, no one will question our doing things together all the time."

"That's true," laughed Emmett. "I had to take Mark to my off base apartment on the weekends at 'A' School."

"You mean the kid that had the hair problem?"

"Yeah. You knew him?"

"Nah," smiled Riley, "Just heard about him. I also heard about the guy that stood up for him one day in the showers."

"Yeah, well that was before we got involved sexually. He was just a nice kid that was too inclined to let himself be picked on. I've always hated bullies, regardless of who they were picking on."

"They said you beat the shit out of the guy."

"Oh, Christ, I hate it when people exaggerate. I hit him once…in the stomach. He got the message. He even apologized to Mark a few weeks later."

Riley laughed. "I figured it was something like that. Barry never looked like he'd gotten beaten up."

"So, are you noisy during sex, Riley?"

"Not usually. I don't know, though. I may have to start using a pillow over my head." He laughed. "That really was great, Emmett. I've never done it that way before."

"The senior called it frottage; some French term." Emmett laughed. "Leave it to a gay guy to know something like that." He paused. "I suppose we should lock the door."

"Already done. Took care of it while you were finishing in the bathroom," answered Riley.

"That's a good thing because…" and Emmett looked pointedly down between them. They were both hard again. He then looked up into Riley's eyes. "God, I love being young and horny."

He skipped the kissing this time and simply reached between them and grabbed Riley's cock as he pushed him onto his back. He began to scoot down the bunk and suddenly realized that the footboard was going to make things difficult, so he slipped off the bunk and pulled Riley's legs over the side of the bunk and spread his legs as Emmett knelt between them.

It'd been nearly a month since he'd had a cock in his mouth and he wasn't inclined to hesitate. He leaned forward and began licking at the slightly leaking head of Riley's cut seven incher as he reached down and began to massage the moderate sized balls beneath.

Riley reached over and pulled the pillow over his face as he let out a groan. He really wanted to be able to let himself enjoy this and the moans and groans helped with that. So best to be cautious and muffle his participation.

Emmett smiled and began working this marvelous weapon into his mouth. Just a little at a time. In an inch, then back out. In an inch and a half, and back out again, always moving slowly. They'd just cum, after all, so this was bound to take a bit of time, so why not simply enjoy it completely?

Riley was squirming a bit by the time Emmett got his nose into his beautiful brown curls. "Oh Christ, Emmett," he moaned.

Emmett reached up with his free hand and began to gently tweak Riley's right nipple. Well that really set the boy off.

"Harder, Emmett."

So he obliged. He squeezed that nipple harder and began to bob a little faster on Riley's cock as he massaged just a bit faster on those balls. This had the effect of really getting Riley moving, his hips bouncing slightly up and down, his torso rolling ever so slight from side to side.

Riley slammed the pillow into his face. "It's coming," he said into it as he thrust his hips up and held them there.

Well, that hadn't taken nearly as long as he'd hoped it would, but Emmett wasn't really going to complain. The hot jism blasted into his mouth and throat. Burst after marvelous burst of sweet, salty, silky goodness. He took six blasts of it before Riley collapsed and simply breathed, hard and fast, as Emmett slowly milked the last few drams of the life producing liquid from the source.

When he was convinced that he had all there was to get, he released the slowly shrinking penis and got up and sat on his knees on the mattress at the foot of the bunk, his back against the footboard. He smiled when Riley finally pulled the pillow off his face and rolled his head to face him.

"That was killer, Emmett!" he whispered harshly. Then he looked down at Emmett's rock hard cock. Riley rolled over and swung his body around and swallowed that cock like a starving man.

The surprise of the move startled Emmett. He had to throw his hand over his mouth. "Oh shit!" he said into it. Jesus, he was so excited. What had happened to control and prolonged enjoyment? He felt his balls begin to pull up almost immediately. He couldn't ever remember being able to cum in such rapid succession. But fuck, what the hell…this rocked.

Riley got to bob maybe six times before he felt Emmett's cock stiffen completely and begin pulsing, pushing volumes of pearly essence up its length and releasing it into Riley's hungry mouth. It'd been almost two months since he'd had a cock in his mouth and he was hungry for this.

Like Emmett, he milked that dwindling member until he couldn't get anything more from it. When he began to sit up and could take note of Emmett, he saw him with his head fallen back as he took in great gulps of air. Riley simply sat up onto his knees and scooted up so that their knees were touching, smiling the whole time.

It took a full minute before Emmett lifted his head and was suddenly looking right into Riley's eyes. They didn't consult in any way other than with those eyes. They moved simultaneously forward and kissed, gently…slowly. This was a kiss of appreciation. As they kissed they moved themselves around and were able to lay once again facing each other, without breaking their kiss. When they did finally separate, it was only to fall fast asleep.

They woke several hours later, having missed lunch at the chow hall. So they got themselves showered, dressed and headed out. They caught the base shuttle bus to the front gate and then walked the short distance to the row of restaurants that always seemed to be nestled up close to any military base. Neither of them was in the mood for fast food, so they chose a low cost restaurant with booths. They got twice the burger and fries for the same money.

Neither was in the mood to return to the base right away, so they simply walked. They stopped at every strip mall they passed and window shopped mostly, only occasionally stopping to buy some small trinket that caught their eye. Oh yeah, and they talked.

They'd shared a bit about their homes over the previous three weeks, but now they shared much more of that life, including their experiences that led to their realization of their orientation. They talked about the struggles of coming to terms with it and how they both managed to keep it well hidden while still satisfying their desires. They discovered that their experiences were pretty similar. Neither had been sex maniacs, but neither had they ever truly been sex starved. There'd been just enough guys over the years to keep their sexual educations moving at a steady pace without it becoming obvious.

Just like Emmett and Mark had done, he and Riley discussed the realities of their expectations, their need to be very cautious and circumspect. And most of all, they couldn't allow themselves to become so attached to one another that their eventual separation would become a major stumbling block to their futures.

Fortunately, the school was a tough one. There was considerable homework and additional studying that had to occur for each of them to learn all there was. It kept them busy enough that the sex was never a driving part of their friendship. The majority of their time together was spent helping each other to understand the material they were being taught.

They took one weekend a month and left the base entirely. Generally, they'd rent a hotel room near one of the amusement parks. Their days they spent in enjoying the entertainments, their nights they spent enjoying each others' bodies fully, unlike the occasional blowjob they'd share at the barracks.

When the day finally arrived for them to leave for their next school, they agreed that they'd had a grand time together. Their farewells were accomplished without tears, just a simple admonishment for each of them to take care to make the most of their careers, however long they lasted.

The final step to becoming a qualified Reactor Operator was something called prototype school. These were shipboard reactors that'd been built on land. Each of the prototype facilities had been built well inland. Emmett was sent to the one in upstate New York. This property contained three reactors. One was identical to an aircraft carrier reactor, one was a submarine type and the third was a new experimental design. The principles were all the same, regardless of size. The only real difference was in the support equipment and the power output of the reactors.

Emmett was assigned to the submarine style of reactor for his practical training, for you see, this school was the one that actually taught the men how to operate what they'd learned about in theory at Nuclear Power School. Not only operate, but also to maintain and test the equipment.

There was no *base* as such. Just a few acres of land set out into the countryside, well away from any human habitation. All that was there were the three reactors and the support buildings. No housing for the sailors. So everyone had to obtain their own living quarters in the towns and country surrounding the site. Emmett hooked up with four other guys he'd known casually at Nuclear Power School. They rented an old farm house that had four bedrooms and a small basement that they made into the fifth bedroom.

What Emmett hadn't known when he hooked up with these four guys was that they were all very religious individuals. This made it a time of enforced chastity for him. It was also moderately humorous for him as his roommates each tried to get him to accept their beliefs. He never revealed his orientation, obviously, so this made it a time of mild frustration for him. It didn't help that the area they were living in was primarily rural with small towns scattered about. No gay community here.

So, what this allowed for, was Emmett being totally committed to the training. He took to it completely, without any outside distractions. With all that dedication, he was the first in his class to qualify. He did it in record time, too. Only four months into the six month school and he was a fully qualified watch stander at the reactor control panel. This meant that he would frequently sit a complete four hour watch at the panel without any senior instructor sitting beside him. He never sat the watch with any of the still unqualified students; he wasn't a qualified instructor, after all.

This made the last two months of the prototype training very relaxing. He'd stand a solo watch once every three days. Otherwise, he would sit with a struggling student and help as much as he could to get them on track for their own qualifications.

The one thing that he was told just before leaving for his first sea tour was that because of his grades at Nuclear Power School and his performance at prototype, his name was going to be placed on the *preferred* list of future instructors. This meant that at the end of his initial three year sea rotation he'd be able to apply for an instructor's slot at either one of those schools and be instantly accepted for a two year teaching billet. Well, that made for interesting options for his future Naval career.

Emmett's first sea going vessel was on a Fleet Ballistic Missile Submarine, or FBM, as it was typically referred to. It was one of the new generation of subs that had been built with a bit more comforts than their predecessors. But the very best thing about his assignment was that his primary port of call was Hawaii. This was where the crew was stationed, but the submarine, or *boat*, was actually located in Guam.

His breaking in period on the new submariner was a bit tough. He had to learn about all the equipment he'd be responsible for, plus he had to learn the intricacies of the submarine systems that related to general functions and safety. It astounded him that he had to have a general knowledge of all the major ships operating systems. He had to be able to recreate some of the system diagrams and flowcharts during his examination board.

The ship qualification took him nearly six months to accomplish. But when he finally passed his board, he was able to proudly wear the 'Dolphins' on his breast that designated him for all time as a U.S. Navy Submariner. He was awfully proud of those dolphins. He was, that is, once his chest recovered.

The ritual aboard submarines was for the already qualified members of the crew to 'tack on' the dolphins of a newly qualified man. That involved having each man ball up his fist and punch the dolphins into your chest. Most of the men were kind and didn't hit all that hard. But there were some that took a fiendish delight in pulling back and giving the punch everything they had, nearly knocking Emmett on his ass.

It took a week for Emmett to begin regaining the feeling on the left side of his chest. But once it was done, it was done.

During all this time, there'd been no sex other than what he accomplished for himself, alone in his shower. The fact that there were numerous cute guys onboard never bothered Emmett. It was a given that the vast majority of them would be heterosexual, and the ones that might be gay were being very careful not to advertise the fact, just like Emmett himself. Still, there was quite a bit of eye candy for his evening showers. The crew's birthing areas on this class of submarine were primarily located in the missile compartment, between the tubes. Each 'cubicle' contained nine bunks and a center table.

Some of the younger guys would change their underwear while lying in their bunks with the curtains closed. But most of the old salts were far less modest and simply let it all hang out. They'd bounce their way to and from the head, their equipment out there for the world to gape at. Of course no one gaped or gawked. That would have been the ultimate in rude. But everyone glanced. It was only natural. There was the usual all guy environment sort of grab assing from time to time, but it was always carefully noncommittal. A slapped ass, or a congenial ribbing about one's equipment. Otherwise, everyone was careful to give their fellow shipmates a bit of room to do their business.

There was one member of Emmett's division that was a character and a half. Carl was a gregarious guy. He managed to always be in a fine mood and was the sort to get the guys around him laughing. He could find a way to have fun with almost everything he did. Even on field day.

Now, that was the day when the entire crew would turn out for four hours and scrub the boat from top to bottom. A submarine was a completely closed environment normally. It absolutely had to be maintained and kept clean. There was far too much sensitive equipment throughout the boat that did not take kindly to dust and dirt. So, once a week everyone broke out the cleaning supplies and attempted to stay ahead of the damaging detritus of any human habitation.

Emmett had been onboard for nearly a year when he began to wonder about Petty Officer First Class Carl Fisher. It was during one of the many weekly field days that Emmett began to notice that Carl seemed to be paying an awful lot of attention to him. Every time Emmett happened to glance Carl's way, there he was, looking at Emmett. And the really odd thing was that he didn't instantly look away. He'd usually simply smile and then turn his attention back to his own task.

Now Carl was not really of the type that Emmett usually thought of in a sexual light. He was slightly overweight and didn't seem to have much in the way of a crotch. Emmett had seen him once in all this time in his underwear and there was what Emmett had come to think of as the typical overweight guy sort of bulge in his briefs; there, but nothing to write home about.

But still, he had the sort of personality that Emmett really enjoyed. When he wasn't cutting up, he was engaging intellectually and he was always there with a helping hand or a bit of advice with the equipment they were responsible for maintaining and operating. The reactor systems were, after all, a bit of a necessity for getting them from point 'A' to point 'B' and back again. So everyone shared their bits of expertise when one of the junior men was struggling. Even Emmett was beginning to take a newbie aside and explain this or that when he saw one of them having a difficulty.

Carl and Emmett didn't socialize away from the boat during that first year or so. There was plenty of time for it, with the schedule that this class of sub usually kept. The two of them just never seemed to be able to strike a balance between the old salt and the newbie.

There were, in fact, two crews for each sub of this type. They'd deploy for approximately three months at a time, each time with only one of the crews. The other crew stayed in Hawaii during what they called the 'off crew' period. The first month of that time was spent on a modified leave. It was a time that no one got charged for so long as you stayed in town and were available to muster twice a week.

Still that first month was always a time of kicking up your heals and enjoying your freedom after three months of being cooped up in an over-large ocean going cigar. The second two months weren't terribly onerous. It was a time to catch up on training and paperwork. Days were usually short. So there was still plenty of time to enjoy life.

The event that changed their perceptions of each other happened onboard during Emmett's second patrol, the period when a crew was at sea for their three month cycle. They were in the chow hall during one of the nightly movies. They'd ended up sitting side by side and had spent the opening half hour of the movie ribbing each other quietly. It happened when Carl said something humorously derogatory that Emmett reached over and flicked his finger into Carl's crotch. Well Carl had jumped and become very quiet for the remainder of the movie.

Well, Emmett figured he'd probably gone a bit too far and what little friendship they had was now over. So he was surprised when Carl held him back after the movie. They sat quietly over a cup of coffee as the chow hall emptied out, everyone else ready to hit their bunks. Carl had selected a table in the far corner of the hall, well away from any of the entrances.

"Man, you flicked the end of my dick, Emmett. How'd you do that?"

"Easy, Carl. I looked for the biggest bulge and aimed for the other side." Carl got a perplexed look on his face at this. "Come on, Carl, everyone knows that overweight guys got a small cock," he laughed. "I figured the bulge was your balls, so I aimed away from them. Didn't think you'd appreciate getting your balls whacked."

Carl finally laughed at this. "Yeah, well, you're not going to go telling the whole world, are you? We fat guys are sensitive to that sort of thing."

"Naw, it'll be our little secret."

"Not that you have that problem," Carl ventured. This conversation was interesting in the extreme. Emmett was a really cute younger guy, but there'd never been any real indication of interest in guys. "Your bulge leaves nothing to the imagination."

Emmett smiled big at this obvious ploy. "Been looking, have you? You're the first to notice." Well, there it was; the opening that could get him into trouble.

Carl took a slow sip of his coffee and simply stared at Emmett. Did he dare? That was definitely a come-on if he'd ever heard one. Still…dared he? But all his instincts told him to go for it, and those instincts had never failed him in the past.

"Not the first. But evidently the first to have the courage to say so."

Emmett laughed softly. "So, I've been missing out, have I? That's not fair, Carl, the old salts are suppose to share these grams of wisdom with the new guys."

Well, that was clear enough. He had to take advantage of this right away, so he spoke up just a touch louder. "So, you want to give me a hand catching up the revisions?"

Emmett caught on to that right away. Carl was in charge of ensuring all the engineering manuals were kept current with revisions. He had a small office in the bottom of the boat, just forward of the engineering spaces, where all the duplicate manuals were kept. It was a tiny little space, with all the manuals in there, but it was big enough for two. Emmett had been there once or twice, helping to move boxes of materials and revisions into it at the beginning of the patrol cycle.

"If you really need the help, sure, I can spare you an hour or two." Emmett did, in fact, have a bit of experience with installing revisions into manuals, since he'd recently been given the responsibility for keeping his division's manuals up to date.

They took the time to finish their coffees quietly. No sense rushing out of the mess hall like two guys off for sex, even if that was precisely what they intended. Appearances…always appearances. It was, after all, the norm for guys to delay the inevitable work that they were saddled with. Oh, no one procrastinated to the point where work was left undone. That would have been stupid. The safety of the entire crew depended on everyone doing their tasks. That didn't mean that you couldn't linger over a coffee before heading off to finish your chores.

Gay men had to always be conscious of the image they projected, so Carl and Emmett made their way to the office, chatting the whole way about what the job entailed. Carl explained that he'd gotten a bit behind and needed to get all the manuals back up to specs as soon as he could. Emmett asked a few salient questions about the process. No one thought anything of it.

Carl motioned Emmett in ahead of him and then entered, turning to close and lock the door behind him. The office was located in the space just forward of the reactor compartment. The three floors contained all the equipment needed to keep the crew in clean air and water. Air scrubbers, desalinization units and spare parts were here. As a result, there wasn't much, if any, traffic through the area. But still, best to lock the door behind them.

When Carl turned around, he found Emmett leaning back against the work surface, smiling. "Nice apartment you have here, Carl."

Carl laughed. "It works in a pinch. Haven't been able to do much in decorating the place. The Engineer would frown on curtains and knick-knacks." The Engineer was the senior officer onboard who had ultimate responsibility for all that happened in the engineering spaces.

They laughed together.

"So," began Emmett, "Is this just going to be a release of convenience, or are you gay too?"

"No," smiled Carl. That was all the information he needed. "I'm gay too." He stepped up so that there wasn't much space between them. "Gods, Emmett, you are cute." He then reached out and cupped the younger man's crotch in his hand.

"Whoosh," said Emmett. "That's nice." He then reached out himself and cupped Carl's crotch in his hand. As he'd thought, there wasn't a big package there. But then, Emmett had never been a size queen. It wasn't the size of the cock that mattered to him. He was much more interested in the size of the personality.

"Disappointed?" asked Carl.

"Not a bit. It's never been about size with me." He closed his eyes and sighed. "Shit, Carl, that feels fabulous. It's been over a year since I've dared."

"Ooh, we can't let that continue," said Carl as he dropped to his knees and began unfastening Emmett's belt and pants.

Emmett could see that Carl had plenty of onboard experience. He knew it because the odd belt used by the military didn't slow him down in the slightest. He only hoped that Carl would not be disappointed by the fact that he wasn't wearing any underwear; he tended not to onboard.

The quick intake of breath by Carl was very satisfying. "Like?" asked Emmett.

"It's gorgeous," whispered Carl. He simply stared at it for a few moments, watching as it began to grow all on its own. It's wasn't that he didn't have enough partners; he certainly did. There were three guys other than Emmett that he frequently shared a few moments. But Emmett had a perfectly complimentary package. This cock was large, as Carl had expected. But the sack below was perfectly sized for the cock they supplied with juices. It was just a marvelous vision of male endowment.

But the admiration needed to end. He slowly reached up and cupped those beautiful orbs in his left hand as he reached for that cock with his right. The cock firmed up immediately as Emmett groaned softly in appreciation. Yes, this was definitely a tool that had seen far too little action recently. The precum began flowing immediately and in such great quantities. This was a cock that wanted satisfaction *now*. The balls beneath didn't hang low for long. They pulled up quickly and tightly to Emmett's groin.

"Oh fuck, Carl!" whispered Emmett harshly. "Oh damn, I can't hold it!" There was real disappointment in that statement.

Carl was only the tiniest bit disappointed by this. But then again, this was so cool too. Or at least it was convenient. He was always taking a chance when he did something like this onboard. There was that slimmest chance that the Engineer would need something from the Log Room, the name this little room had been christened with. There were only two people with keys to this room; Carl and the Engineer.

It had actually happened once, where he'd brought one of his 'friends' to the Log Room and was just about to pull down Robert's pants when they heard someone coming down the ladder just outside the room. Carl had quickly unlocked the door and assumed a working position, as it he were showing Robert something from a manual. The Engineer hadn't said a word, simply come in and gotten the manual he needed and left. It was not unusual for Carl to bring guys down to the Log Room for a bit of extra instruction and help in their qualifications.

So, the fact that Emmett was inclined to be quick in cumming this time, didn't really upset Carl at all. This was the time of the shipboard day when the Engineer was up and about his duties.

Carl took that cock into his mouth and *was* a bit amazed has how much bigger Emmett's cock grew as it prepared for the final event. It wasn't just the head that flared, but the shaft grew as well. Oh, not much, but it was noticeable. And those magnificent orbs got so very tight as to be totally unmovable. It felt as if they too were convulsing with the orgasm that began with a flourish. Oh,

Carl knew this wasn't the way the body worked, but still, it felt like it was happening.

But then his only thought was to swallow as fast as he'd ever had to. That first volley shot straight past his tongue and pounded the back of his throat without stopping to be tasted and savored. Carl tilted his head down slightly so that subsequent emissions would *have* to land on his tongue before continuing their journey. It was quite a satisfying experience for him. A large volume of sweet, salty juices, delivered in huge, pulsing lobs.

When the rush ended, Carl simply milked the shaft, avoiding the over-sensitive head until he was sure he'd cleaned out the remaining dribbles. When he released Emmett's cock and looked up, he saw him smiling down at him.

"That was great, Carl. I only hope next time I can enjoy it longer." Carl smiled up at this. "That is, of course, supposing you're interested in more," smirked Emmett.

"Well, I suppose, if you're going to insist." They laughed softly.

"Ok, I get a chance now," said Emmett as he pulled Carl to his feet and turned him so that he was leaning where Emmett had recently been.

"We'll need to make it quick, Emmett. This is the Engineer's roaming period."

"Gotcha." He dropped to his knees and quickly had Carl's pants and underwear down to his ankles. He wasn't particularly surprised to see that Carl was already fully hard and dripping. It was a testament to how enjoyable it'd been for Carl.

His five and a half inches of tool was nice and fat, which more than made up for the lack of length. The sack was over large for the short cock, but that only meant the potential for quite a bit of return on the effort he was about to put in. Taking Carl's advice to heart, he didn't hesitate; he leaned in and swallowed that fat tube. It was nice, once in a while, to be able to take a cock all the way to the base without having to worry about gag reflex. When you could concentrate your efforts on your partner's sensitivities instead of gagging, things usually resulted in a fine culmination for the recipient.

Emmett put real effort into stimulating Carl. He didn't massage the balls, he tickled them. With his other hand he also tickled that little spot just behind the sack, the perineum, and teased the very edges of his asshole without actually touching it. That, combined with the tongue action he was giving the glans soon had Carl writhing in anticipation.

If they were anywhere but the boat, Carl would have done his very best to ignore some of what Emmett was doing, but this was neither the time or place for that, so he just let his excitement overflow and it wasn't more than five minutes before he was spewing his seed into that marvelous mouth.

To Emmett's delight, Carl wasn't a heavy shooter. His was a more leisurely flow from the slit, which landed directly onto his tongue, allowing him to savor the emissions. The quiet groans and moans from above him was more than enough indication of enjoyment. He smiled as he swallowed the goodly quantity of jism. A fine little snack just before bunk time.

He meticulously cleaned that cock before pulling Carl's pants up so that he could put himself back together while Emmett did the same thing as he stood.

"Whew, that was great, Emmett," said Carl with a warm, appreciative smile.

"It was great for me too, Carl. Been too long for me."

"Well, we'll see if we can't get together a bit more."

"Cool. Now, do you really want a little help with your work down here?"

"Actually, yes. There was quite a load up for the component manuals. I've got all the Reactor Plant Manuals up to date, but these individual manuals have fallen behind."

They agreed to get together over the next few days for a couple of hours to try and get the work caught up. They didn't engage in sex every time they got together, but they did when they were fairly certain of privacy. The blowjobs that resulted were much more prolonged and really worked to cement their friendship.

Carl never did introduce Emmett to his other boys during that patrol. And Emmett never asked. It was enough to be able to satisfy his itch with Carl every few days or so.

Work and watches continued without interruption as they drew nearer and nearer to patrol's end. It was a much more relaxed period for Emmett, now that he had a place he could go to get a little sexual enjoyment from time to time.

When they arrived back in Hawaii, Emmett and his two roommates took possession of the house they rented during the off crew. It was a house that was rented by three of the men from the other crew during *their* off crew. It was a very convenient arrangement, knowing that they didn't have to look for new housing each time they came off patrol. This place was about fifteen minutes north of Pearl City, out near Wahiawa.

Emmett's two roommates were both heterosexual as far as he knew, and they had no clue that he was any different. They got along well because all three of them were quiet individuals and not into the continual partying that many of their shipmates engaged in during their free time.

The one activity they shared in common was their enjoyment of golf. Actually, it was a passion of Eric's. Emmett and Bill had simply been bored one day and had suggested that Eric teach them golf. That was all the prompting that Eric needed. It was mere coincidence that there was a fine golf course not two minutes from their house. None of them were very good, but that wasn't the point. The point was getting out of the house, getting a little exercise and enjoying the sunny Hawaiian days.

The entire crew had to get dressed in their summer whites twice a week and drive into Pearl Harbor and muster. It never lasted more than half an hour. It was simply a time for the officers to ensure that no one had skipped town on an unauthorized leave and to put out any announcements. It was at the second of these musters that Carl came up to Emmett after everyone had been dismissed.

"Hey, Emmett, got any plans for the next couple of days?"

"Nothing that can't be set aside, just more golf."

"Golf? You?"

"Yeah, well it's something to do that doesn't involve getting rip-roaring, falling down drunk. Have you looked into the eyes of some of these guys?"

Carl laughed at that. "No, I try not to. If I did, I'd probably laugh myself into insensibility. Some of these guys will never grow up."

"That's the truth. So, what did you have in mind?"

"Well, I was planning on having a pool party at my house for the next couple of days; just a few guys and lots of food."

"Pool?"

"Yeah, I rent this place precisely because of the pool. So, you interested?"

"Hell yeah I'm interested. When?"

"Now."

"Ok, I'll just run home and pick up a few things."

"You won't need anything, Emmett. This is a clothing optional party," he said softly then smiled big. "Actually, it's a clothing forbidden party," he whispered.

Well that had just all sorts of possibilities. Emmett had no problem interpreting Carl's intentions, and he was all for it. He'd never before had the chance to be with a group of like-minded individuals. The idea of a nudist camp had always fascinated Emmett, but he'd never known where to find one. This idea of spending a couple of days in that type of environment was exciting in the extreme. Especially if it was just guys.

All Emmett had to do was tell his roommates that he wouldn't be riding home with them and that he'd ride back with them at the next muster. With that arranged, he let Carl drive him to his house and a couple days of heaven.

"I presume I'll know these guys?" asked Emmett as they left the parking lot.

"Oh yes." Carl's smile got huge. "Oh, and they have no idea who I'm bringing along today. They just know that I'm bringing a new recruit."

"New recruit, am I?" Emmett laughed. "Sounds like I'm joining some new secret organization."

Carl laughed at that. "Well, I suppose it is at that. Can't let out that we're all into guys."

"That works. Am I going to have to worry about imposing on relationships?"

"Nope. We're all in this for the fun. No one's allowed to fall in love. We mix and match at will."

"Hell, Carl, Hawaii really is paradise."

Carl drove up into the hills of Pearl City. He drove up and up and up, until Emmett was sure they'd soon be surrounded by cloud cover.

"Jesus, Carl, you got a personal appointment with God or something?"

Carl laughed hard at this. "Good one. Not God, just heaven. You'll see in just a bit."

The higher they got into the hills the more spread out the homes became, until finally Carl pulled into a drive that took them back well off the road. Nestled there was a fine looking, well appointed home. It was a single story affair and looked totally Hawaiian. There was lots of decorative thatching and several Hawaiian themed statues.

"Jesus, Carl, how can you afford something like this?"

"It belongs to a family friend. Lots of money. We have an arrangement that allows me to use it during my off crews and they schedule their vacations for my patrol periods."

"Lucky guy. It's beautiful, Carl."

"Wait 'til you see the inside. You might take note of the fact that there isn't another house in visible range. Makes going au-natural simple."

Well that prospect set the butterflies loose in Emmett's stomach.

"The rest of the guys aren't showing up until afternoon. That'll give me the chance to show you where everything is. Do you cook?"

That question, out of the blue, caused Emmett's mind to stumble. "Uh, yeah, I cook."

"Great! The rest of the guys are hopeless in the kitchen. I could use some help. Can you do more than boil eggs?"

"Eggs can be boiled?" teased Emmett.

"Oh God."

"Seriously, I try as many of those Food Network recipes as I can. Emeril Lagasse and Bobby Flay are my heroes."

Carl got really excited at this. "Oh this is going to be so killer. I'll show you around then we'll look in the kitchen and decide what we'll cook. Then we can go to the store for the things we're missing."

"With all these naked male bodies, are we going to have time to eat?"

"Oh, absolutely. We're going to have to eat regularly to keep up our strength."

The house tour revealed a veritable mansion on a single floor. The house was a horseshoe shaped affair that wrapped toward the back, so the view from the drive was very deceiving. There were six bedrooms, three down each leg of the horseshoe. Each of them was well decorated and very large. The pool was nestled inside the legs of the shoe so that privacy was not an issue.

It didn't take long for the tour and even less time for the menu selection. Since Emmett had professed a love of Bobby Flay's outdoor grilling menus, he was nominated to be the primary chef for the weekend. Their trip to the store was a relatively quick one as they didn't have much beyond fresh meat, fish and seafood to get. They were home in plenty of time to pack everything away and strip down before the rest of Carl's guests arrived. They even had time enough to simply lounge beside the pool with a glass of chilled Chardonnay.

When the first guest arrived, Emmett was only aware of it because suddenly there was a body stepping around the lounges to have a look at him. And what a body, even clothed. But then, Emmett had always admired this particular body. It was Robert.

Well, Emmett's mouth fell open. This was absolutely the last person he'd expected to see here. Robert was one of the nuclear trained electricians, so they saw each other frequently as they went about their tasks in the same spaces. He was a year younger than

Emmett and absolutely stunning. What caused Emmett's surprise is that Robert was engaged to be married.

"Hi, Emmett," he smiled. "I gather you weren't expecting me."

"Uh, no. I'm still not sure I'm seeing right. You are the same Robert that's engaged to get married next year, aren't you?"

"Oh yes," laughed Robert. "That hasn't changed. But hey, what can I say, I like guys too."

Well if Emmett was going to be spending a couple of days with naked guys, this was certainly one he would have wanted to have around. Robert always gave you the impression that he was built well. His clothes fit just tight enough to let you know that there wasn't an ounce of fat on his body. His black hair and well tanned complexion gave him a bit of an exotic look. Of course, the most unclothed Emmett had ever seen him was in t-shirt and pants. But that t-shirt had been tight and the sculpted body beneath was clearly visible.

Carl hopped up at that point and hugged and kissed Robert… full on the lips. And Robert didn't hesitate, he returned as good as he got. When they broke apart, Robert simply smiled down at Emmett and stepped up and leaned over and gave him an equally passionate kiss.

"Come on, Emmett, get over it," he said softly. "The next couple of days are going to be fun, but only if you stop reacting like a stunned fish." He then stood up and walked back into the house.

"He's right, you know," said Carl.

Emmett chuckled. "I know, you're right. But hell, of all the guys I could imagine being here for this, he was the very last one on my list."

Carl laughed back at him. "Yeah, I can imagine. All right, the other two are Clayton and Bradford. This will give you a chance to get used to the idea."

"Clayton from the communications shack?" Carl nodded. "Bradford, the new seaman?" Another nod. "You certainly spread your interest around. Is Bradford as naïve as he comes off?"

"Definitely not. He just never learned how to protect himself from discovery. How he's made it this long without someone figuring him out is beyond me. I've been working with him. Trying to help him tone down the effeminate side of himself."

"Well, I think it's working. I've noticed a change."

"That's good," said a very young voice from behind him.

Bradford was all of eighteen and a few months, and he definitely had that lost young puppy dog look to him. He was the sort of boy you wanted to wrap up in your arms and simply protect from the depredations of the world.

When Emmett turned around he could definitely feel the stirrings of protectiveness. If anything, Bradford was even more the lost puppy in his civilian clothes and away from the macho crew environment. His very blond hair was an unruly mess, despite the shortness of it. He'd obviously driven here with the windows open on his car. He was almost too skinny. Emmett was looking forward to seeing what the boy looked like unclothed.

"Damn, Emmett, you remind me so much of my neighbor back home."

Emmett stood and walked over to the boy. He immediately wrapped him in an embrace. "Ah, but would your neighbor have hugged you like this?"

Bradford laughed at this. "Not until I was naked."

"Ooh, lucky neighbor." He then ventured a quick kiss which Bradford returned willingly. "Well, far be it for me to disillusion you," said Emmett. "Go get naked, Bradford."

"Just Brad, Emmett." He then headed for the bedroom area.

"My turn," said a new voice.

Emmett turned slightly and, sure enough, there was Clayton. He was the oldest of them, being twenty-seven. He'd been in the Navy for eight years and Emmett knew he was thinking of making it a career. He was handsome, without being gorgeous. He'd never seen Clayton in civvies either, so the he was pleasantly surprised by the casual elegance of the man. His dark brown hair was curly, even in the short style dictated by the military. Actually, Emmett always suspected that there was some ethnic heritage in the man's background. His skin was a bit darker than most and it never seemed to alter in tone, even after two months at sea. That implied no need to work on his tan.

Clayton came to Emmett and pulled him into an embrace and gave him a very thorough kiss. "Gods, I've wanted to do that to you since the first day you came aboard. Welcome to the club, Emmett."

"Thanks, Clayton."

"Clay, in this company."

"So, go get comfortable," said Carl. "Emmett and I will stir up lunch for everyone."

Actually, Emmett and Carl had already put a couple of platters together for a grab and snack sort of lunch around the pool. There was one large platter of sliced fruits, another with cheese and crackers, and then a third with various meats and sausages. Once they'd set these out on the poolside buffet, they went in and pulled two bottles of chilled wine from the wine cooler; another bottle of the Chardonnay and a Riesling. These they opened and put into buckets of ice to keep them chilled.

"Brad really likes wine?" asked Emmett as the two of them put together small plates of snacks for themselves.

"Yes I do," answered Brad as he and Robert came out of the house. "Not all us country guys are beer belching morons," he laughed as he poured himself a bit of the Riesling.

Emmett was very pleased to see that Robert was just as endowed as he'd imagined. Brad on the other hand was more modestly hung. Perhaps six and a half or seven slim inches. Still, his nuts were plenty big enough, and the very blond hair on Brad's head extended to his crotch as well. That sort of surprised Emmett. All the blond guys he'd met or seen in the past had darker pubic hair than was on their heads. Brad was very blond all over, with just a touch of hair on his chest.

"You like?" asked Brad with just a touch of a blush. Although he was less of the effeminate than he'd been, it was obvious that he was still just a touch shy and unsure of himself.

Emmett smiled. "As a matter of fact I do. Sorry to stare, I've just never met anyone that's as blond all over as you are."

"Really?"

"It's true. All the blonds I've ever seen have had much browner hair in their crotch."

"Huh," was the boy's only response as he turned to fill a plate for himself.

Robert, on the other hand, had already filled a plate and was seated on a lounge chair with a glass of wine on the side table.

Emmett looked openly as he took the lounge next to Robert. The guy's dark brown hair extended everywhere on his body. He wasn't a bear, as such, but his hair extended to several parts of his body. His lower legs and forearms were pleasantly brown as was the chest area just between his pecs. His crotch had quite a full compliment of hair. It also looked very soft, if that were possible. It didn't have that coarse look that most guys had. The hair there was so much longer than Emmett was used to seeing.

"So, Emmett, how long have you known you were gay?" asked Robert.

That set them off into a discussion of their experiences growing up. It really was a very nice way to begin their two day odyssey. There was nothing like getting acquainted by talking about the intimate parts of your lives to really get acquainted and comfortable with each other. It also helped a lot to know that one of them had any particular ghosts lingering back there. No one had to worry about offending inadvertently.

Even Brad, who'd grown up in a rural environment had been fortunate in that he'd met the next door neighbor's sixteen year old son when Brad had been thirteen. It'd been about experimentation for Brad while receiving instruction from the older boy. It had allowed Brad to explore his feelings without being found out by his peers. The older boy had been completely supportive until he'd turned eighteen and then had made it clear that they could not continue their intimate relationship.

Of course, by this time, Brad had made the acquaintance of a school mate of like mind and they'd kept company for the final years of their educations. What made Brad so hesitant and just a touch naïve was that he'd only grown up with the two sexual partners, and never around any sort of gay support groups. He'd joined the Navy for the education and a career away from rural life.

Clay's story was totally different. He'd grown up in San Diego and his feelings had never been questioned. His was a rare relationship with his parents. They were disappointed in his choice, but had not rejected him for it. There had been no particular encouragement of his chosen way of life, but neither had there been ridicule. They'd been good parents that had provided him with the parental affection he needed and allowed him enough freedom to safely explore for himself. They'd always ensured his safety and often questioned him about where he was going and who he was with.

Robert had grown up in Wisconsin, a little town named LaCrosse, on the western border of the state, next to the Mississippi River. It had a population of about fifty thousand. Robert had no idea if there was any sort of gay community. He'd never been the least interested in a sexual relationship with another guy…until he joined the Navy, that is. It was during Electricians 'A' School, in Great Lakes that he'd discovered the enjoyment that only another guy could give. It'd happened with his roommate. Since then he'd discovered that he enjoyed sex with both sexes because each satisfied something different within him.

Carl was twenty-five and he'd joined the Navy right out of high school. His was the typical story of the overweight kid that none of the girls wanted to date. It didn't help that he was extremely intelligent and found education to be a wonderful challenge and could always be found with his nose buried in a book. As a result of this, his social skills were rudimentary at best and pathetic at worst. It wasn't until he'd gotten into the Navy that he learned how to interact with the world around him and he learned about the joys of male to male sex. He was a devotee after his first experience in boot camp.

It was a very fine first hour of their gathering. Everyone was much more relaxed with Emmett's presence. The next logical step in their gathering was, of course, staring at them from the court between the home's wings…the pool. It began as leisurely swimming and floating off the results of their lunch and slowly degenerated into a half hour of rough housing that entailed a considerable amount of crotch and ass grabbing. It wasn't long before they were all sporting full fledged erections.

Emmett wasn't sure how it happened exactly. Suddenly Brad was leading him by the hand to the shallow end of the pool. Emmett hadn't noticed any sort of consultation about the matter, but there also seemed to be no objections. Once there, Brad gently pushed Emmett onto the steps.

This was obviously a completely custom pool because the steps covered the entire width of the pool at his end. They were also wider, as in, each tread was nearly three feet deep. And the rise of each step was four inches at the most. What this meant was that when Emmett sat down, there was plenty of room for his ass and when he was pushed back onto the next higher step it wasn't really uncomfortable. He didn't have the sharp edge of the next step digging into this back. That was aided by the fact that the front edge of the steps had been molded with a large bull nose edge detail.

Brad had obviously done this before because he knew precisely which step to sit Emmett on. The water only covered about half of his ass cheeks as he lay back and Brad gently pushed Emmett's legs apart to assume a position between them.

"Kind of a take charge sort of guy, eh?" asked Emmett with and smile and chuckle.

Brad looked up and smiled. "Sometimes."

"Well, don't let me stop you."

Brad chuckled and leaned forward and simply began licking at the head of Emmett's damp tool, grabbing the base of it to hold it steady.

Emmett simply leaned back onto his elbows and let his head fall back. This was, after all, the ultimate purpose of this little get together, so he was just going to let it all hang out and enjoy whatever came along. Having this handsome young blond boy between his legs was a definite turn on and a hell of a way to begin it all.

Brad could hardly believe where he was at this moment. This was only the second time he'd been invited over to Carl's. The other time, it'd just been him, Carl and Clay. To have Robert and Emmett here was going to make this a marvelous two days. After all, Brad liked his cocks a bit bigger than Carl and Clay. These two new guys definitely fit the bill. It'd been nearly a year since he'd left home, losing his access to those two magnificent pieces of manhood at home.

But Robert and Emmett were just as long and fat as the guys he'd learned from. And he was bound and determined to take his time and enjoy them. Emmett got to be first by the simple expedient that he'd been the nearest of the two when Brad decided that he couldn't wait any longer.

He didn't rush this at all. He simply licked at that perfect mushroom, getting it well lubricated, while his hand caressed the base of Emmett's shaft, gently rubbing the modest bush. Oh this was marvelous. So clean and so very manly.

Carl and Clay had just a touch of the feminine about them. Robert he'd only known a short time, but he certainly did not exhibit any girlish traits. But Emmett had always seemed to Brad to be so very, very manly.

Brad knew that he came off as more effeminate than was probably wise, but he couldn't help himself. It's just the way he felt about himself. It wasn't an attempt to put his sexual preferences out on front street to shock everyone, because that would have been suicide to any military career. He just hadn't known how to tone it down…until Carl had taken him under his wing and made some suggestions.

Carl had confessed to him that he was also inclined to be much more effeminate than was truly wise in the military environment. He had to work constantly to tone himself down…had to always be conscious of the image he was projecting. It'd made a big difference to Brad, having the older guy giving him helpful advice.

But here was this very manly man before him, willingly allowing Brad to minister to the needs that every man had. And not just willing, but apparently eager.

"Ooh, we're going to have to ask Carl to extend this party."

"Yeah? How long?" asked Brad.

"Oh, I was thinking about another year of what you're doing will be just about right."

Brad's answer was simple and direct. He wrapped his lips around the head of the mushroom and slowly worked it into his mouth.

"Oh God, yes!" groaned Emmett.

Brad glanced up and smiled. There was nothing like the sound of a man enjoying what he was doing.

Just as he thought that, Brad felt someone place their hands on his ass cheeks and begin rubbing them. Oh, that was hot! He moaned his enjoyment of the attention. He also noticed that Robert leaned up and whispered into Emmett's ear, to which Emmett nodded. Then Clay was obstructing Brad's view of Emmett's head by leaning in to begin nibbling at Emmett's right nipple.

Robert moved down to Brad's right side and did something. Suddenly Emmett was pulling his legs out of the water and set them on Brad's shoulders.

Oh shit, Emmett was in heaven. Brad on his cock, Clay on his nipples, and now Robert was willing to play with his asshole. He wasn't sure how far Robert intended to go, but whatever he did would simply blow this experience out of the park.

Emmett reached up and placed a hand on the back of Clay's head and pushed him down gently. Clay got the message and began to work at that nipple with much more determination. And then Emmett felt Robert's finger begin tracing its way up his crack and then begin massaging his hungry, neglected, sphincter.

"Mmmm!"

Brad was in his own piece of heaven. The process of elimination was a simple one. Carl was back there playing with his ass.

Carl knew how much Brad loved having his ass played with and getting fucked, so he was going to give the boy what he wanted. As he massaged those beautiful young orbs, he knelt down into the water and began to work those cheeks apart until he was granted complete access to the joys inside. He then leaned forward and put his face between those cheeks and stabbed his tongue at that tight little pucker.

Well that got a loud groan out of the youngster, which in turn elicited a moan from Emmett as the vibration on his cock sent a new wave of excitement through him.

Robert was smiling to himself as he worked his finger over Emmett's hot man hole. It didn't take any time at all before it relaxed and he was able to begin pushing at the threshold. There was no resistance to this and his middle finger slipped right inside, all the way to his fist. Oh, this hole definitely wanted some attention.

Emmett nearly exploded when Robert's finger entered him. It'd been quite some time since anything or anyone had entered through that door and he hadn't realized how much he'd missed it… until now. Oh that finger felt magnificent. It felt even better when Robert started to slowly fuck him with it.

"Oh hell," he breathed.

Brad was just as eager for similar attention. He allowed his ass to relax completely as he began to bob up and down on Emmett's now leaking tool. Oh that taste of man fluid was marvelous. Nothing compared to the taste of the elixir that could only be gotten one way. Brad could now feel that Robert had his hand between Emmett's cheeks and that only caused this remarkable cock to stiffen even more in his mouth. The flow increased correspondingly.

The minute Brad loosened up, Carl wasted no time. He removed his face and put two fingers up against that little bit of glory, knowing full well that Brad would take them both without any hesitation or resistance. He pushed, and sure enough, in they slipped. He reached between the boy's legs at the same time and took a firm hold on Brad's rock hard, leaking cock.

"Mmmmm…Arrrrrg!" groaned Brad. Oh shit, that felt fantastic!

Emmett began to writhe as this blond bomber vibrated his cock again. Fuck, he'd never experienced this sort of attention before. Three guys hitting all of his most sensitive hot spots at the same time. It was a wonder that he was lasting as long as he was. But the tingling began soon enough.

"Oh God, guys, oh God..."

Brad knew what that meant. Of course the fact that the cock in his mouth seemed to grow three sizes in a few short seconds was all the warning he needed. Brad began to push back and forth with intensity. He was just as close as Emmett was and he desperately wanted to cum at the same time. Emmett's first blast hit the back of Brad's throat and that was all it took to send *him* over the edge.

Carl could feel Brad's orgasm, both as his cock pumped in his fist and as his asshole clinched like a vice onto Carl's two fingers. He glanced around and could also see the boy swallowing and bobbing with a vengeance. Since Carl had some experience with Emmett's rather large loads, he knew exactly what the boy was getting. He smiled.

Robert was just about to insert a second finger into Emmett's ass when his finger was suddenly grabbed and seemed to get sucked into that hot orifice.

Clay was forced down onto Emmett's nipple by the hand on his head, and so he really attacked it with his tongue and teeth.

"Oh...damn...Damn...DAMN!" yelled Emmett, as he arched his back.

And he did yell. It was a good thing that the neighbors were so distant, thought Carl, with a smile.

It was like no orgasm he'd ever had. Of course, he'd never had three guys working him over at the same time before. It was the most incredible experience of his life as his cock throbbed and throbbed and pulsed so hard that it was very nearly painful to endure. But enjoy it he did as the fireworks exploded behind his shut eyes and every nerve caught fire. This orgasm reached the tips of his toes, he was tingling so hard.

When he finally hit that wall that meant there was no more to give, he collapsed completely and utterly. He was flat played out, that had been so intense. The only action he could manage was to continue breathing...hard, and fast. He had no strength for anything else.

Brad wasn't in much better shape. He'd never experienced anything like this. To have someone getting him off while he was seeing to someone else's needs was the most incredible thing that he'd ever experienced sexually. When he finally felt Emmett collapse, he did the same thing, his own cock fully emptied.

Carl had been expecting this so he gently lowered Brad's exhausted body down until he was lying stretched out in the pool with only his head and shoulders out of the water and on top of Emmett.

"Damn!" cried Clay. "That was fucking HOT!"

All Emmett and Brad could manage as a response was to smile. Both were breathing too heavy to manage any sort of coherent reply to that. Hell, they couldn't even manage a chuckle.

Carl and Robert simultaneously removed their fingers from the respective holes, which incredibly elicited two loud moans of displeasure. Then the three helpers simply looked at one another and chuckled. Yes, that had been a stupendous beginning to their holiday together. But the three of them were all on the verge after what they'd witnessed, so they simply stood where they were and each began to jack themselves off, watching each other as they did so.

Carl was the first to let fly as his cum flew up onto Brad's back. Robert wasn't more than a couple of moments behind him. As he came, he twisted his body slightly so that his ropes of cum landed on both Brad and Emmett. Clay was the last to groan in pleasure as he let his seed release onto Emmett's chest and Brad's head.

After they'd each cum, the three helpers simply laid back into the water and floated out into the center of the pool and toward one side, where they gathered together, holding themselves up at the edge of the pool.

"Fuck, you'd think we'd planned that," said Clay. "Man, that was better than the time you and I ganged up on Brad, Carl."

"I couldn't believe Brad took the initiative this time," laughed Carl. "I'm so proud of him."

"Yeah, that was certainly out of character," said Clay. "Your lessons seem to be paying off, Carl."

"I've been trying."

"To see them get off at the same time was killer," said Robert, just a touch of awe in his voice.

"You know," said Carl, "What really surprised me was that Brad was able to take all of Emmett's load without losing a drop."

Robert's eyebrows rose at this. "It's that big?"

"Oh God yes. *I* nearly choked on it the first time he came in my mouth."

"Whoa!" said Clay. "That's got to be impressive. You've got the fastest mouth onboard."

"Why thank you, Clay. That's the nicest thing you've ever said to me," he laughed.

Just then they saw the two objects of their fun start to get out of the pool.

"Oh I see how it is," called Carl. "One pop and you're off."

The two of them turned to face the pool, putting an arm around each others' waist.

"Yeah, well it seems that somebody made a mess all over us," said Emmett, Brad smiling like a Cheshire cat beside him. "I *am not* going to rinse off in the pool and have to swim in this stuff the rest of the day." With that, the two turned and entered the house, heading toward the bedrooms, the sound of raucous laughter following behind them.

"Thanks Emmett," said Brad as they turned into the bathroom of the left wing.

"Shit, Brad, what are you thanking me for? You're the one that did all the work. That was awesome, by the way."

"You didn't pull away when I started dragging you to the end of the pool." He got very shy suddenly. "That's the first time I've ever done that."

"I know you don't mean the blowjob."

"No. It's the first time I've initiated the sex."

"Really?"

"Uh huh," Brad answered, blushing. "Carl's always telling me I need to be more assertive, take a chance."

"Well no need to be embarrassed, Brad," said Emmett, pulling the boy into an embrace. He then reached up and lifted Brad's face and gave him a kiss of genuine appreciation. It was a marvelous kiss, too. Both of them immediately opened their mouths and began exploring each others' mouth, gently, even lovingly. When they finally broke after a couple of minutes, Emmett saw the tears in Brad's eyes. "Hey, buddy, you done great. I think the best part is that is was so unexpected. Now, why the tears?"

"Just happy, that's all," answered Brad with a huge grin. "Just happy. Now, could we please wash all this slimy shit off our bodies?"

They climbed into the shower together and spent the next fifteen minutes washing each other off, being certain to reach each and every crack and crevice on the others' body. Emmett was easily able to remain unexcited, he'd cum so hard, but Brad was a typical teenager, he got hard almost immediately.

"Jesus, Brad, you got a license for that weapon?" laughed Emmett as he grabbed hold and began to stroke the younger man's cock.

"I can't help it, Emmett. You're just too hot, and I'm always fucking horny."

Emmett chuckled for a moment and then looked closely at the object of his attention. He decided rather quickly that it looked perfect.

"You know what I'd really like?"

"What?"

"You think I could convince you to fuck me with that thing?"

Brad's eyes widened immediately. "Really?"

"Yeah, really. It's just the size I like. Slender and not too long. I've never liked long, fat, or long and fat cocks inside me. But this," he squeezed Brad's cock, "is just right."

"I...I've never been the top before, Emmett."

"Never? Well, it's about time you had the chance to experience the other side of life. I can go both ways, but I really prefer the bottom." He looked up and smiled and the shocked boy. "Could I convince you to give it a try? I'd really like it."

"Yeah, sure, I'd love to try."

"Just remember the times it was the best for you and try to duplicate it. I'll let you know if it's not right for me." With that, Emmett turned around and bent over. "Come on baby, let's see what you have left."

Brad grabbed the bottle of hair conditioner and quickly lubed up his cock and then he took his time, feeling his way along Emmett's crack, spending a bit more time with each pass simply massaging Emmett's pucker. With each pass Emmett pushed further and further back, until Brad was forced to finally push his index finger into that hot little hole.

"Oh damn, Brad, that's great. But I'm already a bit loose. Use two."

Well, what the hell, Emmett was the leader here, so Brad did as he was asked and pushed a second finger inside. The two fingers moved smoothly inside with very little resistance. But he spent several moments simply working them back and forth, turning them slightly as he finger fucked Emmett.

Oh God, that felt good. Emmett hadn't had anything but his own finger in his ass since he and Mark had separated at 'A' School. Riley had been a total bottom and couldn't perform at all as a top. So he'd been forced to do without. This was heaven. Of course it didn't hurt that it was this handsome teenager doing the deed. But, as much as he was enjoying this, he wanted more.

"Please, Brad, now. I want you inside me."

"But that's only two fingers," objected Brad. "I was told it had to be three."

"Don't sweat it, Brad. I can handle it. You're not that big. Trust me."

Well, since his experience was all on the receiving end, Brad just had to trust that Emmett knew what he was doing. He gently pulled his fingers out and positioned himself. He remembered to use his hands to spread Emmett's cheeks as far open as they'd go and then began to slowly push forward, determined to take his time, knowing how much that first entry could hurt.

But Emmett wasn't having any of that. He jutted his hips backward slightly, forcing Brad's head past the threshold, along with about an inch of shaft. Then he held steady as he let the sharp stab of pain diminish.

"Whew," he said finally. "All right, that's the hard part. The pain's gone now, Brad. I'm all yours."

So Brad began the slow process of working his entire cock inside Emmett's body, remembering how he'd always appreciated the man that took his time. What surprised him was how hot it was inside there. He'd never imagined that doing this could be so damn hot. Of course, no one had ever offered him the chance. All anyone wanted to do was fuck him. This was totally new. The idea that another man wanted to share the sexual experience totally was totally freaking cool.

"Oh damn, Brad," breathed Emmett, "That is just so fucking awesome. Oh God, get it all inside before I die of pleasure." With that he pushed back, forcing the entire length of Brad's cock inside him. "Oh yeah," he moaned, "That's the spot. Oh damn that is just so fucking incredible. Come on Brad, do it now. Let me feel you cum inside me."

Well, that wasn't going to take much. That last push had nearly sent him over the edge as it was. What had felt so hot before was now a furnace. He began to pull out and then back in, lengthening his stroke each time. It wasn't but a moment or two before he was giving full strokes to that incredible body under him.

As he began to gain confidence and started to increase the speed, Emmett did something that made it impossible for Brad to prolong the experience…he began to clinch his asshole on each out stroke.

"Oh fuck, Emmett, I can't hold it any longer," he moaned.

"Go for it, baby. Fill me up. Come on, pound it in there." Emmett immediately began to move back and forth more rapidly and soon it was paycheck time.

Brad tried his best to hold out, but the increased speed and clinching sphincter did their work. God, it felt like the head of his cock was going to explode and his balls were so tightly pulled up into his crotch that he could actually feel the strain.

"Ahhhh!" he yelled as he exploded into that oven of delight. He grabbed Emmett's waist with all his might and pulled him one final time into his groin and held him there as his cock blew its contents deep into his new friend. Damn, the jets of cum felt like they were releasing with such force that the cum would surely reach Emmett's heart…maybe further. His whole body spasmed as the orgasm just went on and on and on.

When it finally, gratefully ended, he moaned as he collapsed onto Emmett's back and simply let his arms hang down. "Ooohhh," he breathed.

Emmett, once he'd regained his senses, reached down and grabbed the boy's hands and pulled them up and held them tightly to his chest, forcing Brad to stay in position. That had been incredible. He'd forgotten what an incredible pleasure that could be. But feeling that cock expand inside and then pulse out its juices had been a truly fine climax to what had begun in the pool. He was now truly grateful for the staying power that only a teenage cock could manage. What a marvelous dessert course after the main event.

Emmett held those arms tightly to him until he finally felt the disappointing withdraw of Brad's softened penis as it slipped out on its own.

"How you doing back there?"

"Huh? Oh sorry," whispered Brad as he slowly slipped off Emmett's back and onto his knees in the tub.

Emmett turned and knelt in front of the visibly exhausted boy and simply held him as he continued to recover. It wasn't long before the results of their loving was finding its way back out the way it had gone in.

"Brad, that was exquisite," whispered Emmett.

Brad's immediate response was to fling his arms around Emmett and hug him tightly. "Oh Emmett, that was incredible. I didn't know that would feel so great." Then he began to weep softly. "No one's ever offered to let me do that."

Emmett understood what the poor lad was feeling. "That's the way it should always be, Brad. Good sex is about a complete sharing. Everyone gets to participate in all the great stuff. Sex should be mutually satisfying." He gave Brad a squeeze. "That was awesome, by the way. Thanks."

"Thank *you*," he answered as he leaned back and started to get up. "Now, can we try this shower thing again? I think I'll wash myself, though. I'm not taking a chance that you'll get me all excited again." He chuckled. "I think I hurt down there right now." He then looked pointedly down at his deflated member. "Well, that's a relief. I wasn't sure it was all still there. Felt like the head got blasted off."

Well, that set them both off into gales of laughter, which continued until they'd washed themselves a second time and were drying themselves off. When they finally rejoined the others, the three of them were once again on the lounges and snacking a bit more.

"What the fuck was all the noise about?" asked Clay as they entered the pool area.

"Ah, just helping Brad here reach escape velocity." The two of them broke up into laughter again as they moved to the buffet to pour themselves another glass of wine.

"Well, if what we heard is any indication," said Carl with a chuckle, "I think he made it."

"Oh yeah," said Brad, with real enthusiasm. Then he sobered. "Emmett let me give him anal intercourse."

"You fucked him?" asked Robert.

"No," he answered quite seriously as he took one of the vacant lounges. "We engaged in anal sex and he let me be the top. I think calling it a fuck is just too crude for what I just experienced."

There was silence for several moments as they digested that bit of logic.

"Sorry," said Robert. "Didn't mean to be crude."

"Hey, no sorry," said Brad. "It's probably the right word most of the time. It just didn't feel right for this."

"Jesus, now he's turning into a philosopher," laughed Carl.

That broke the tension as they all busted up into laughter.

"Ok," said Brad after everyone had calmed a bit. "Sorry, didn't mean to get all serious. It was just so unexpected…and so awesome."

"I had no idea you liked that, Emmett," said Carl. "You never mentioned it."

"Sorry, Carl, but I never mentioned it because I'm awful particular about who I do it with. I'm a bit of a size queen." He laughed. "Only thinner cocks get to go there. The rest of you guys are far too fat. Sorry."

"Well, that certainly simplifies any speculation," said Clay matter of factly.

Robert, Carl and Clay exchanged favors over the next three hours, but Brad and Emmett made it quite clear that they were exhausted and needed time to regain their feeling again. In fact, they both fell asleep in their loungers for an hour. Fortunately, that part of the court was in shade by that time of day, so neither of them suffered by laying in the sun over long.

At four, Carl and Emmett retired to the kitchen to begin dinner preparations. They'd decided to go all out. Emmett would prepare a remarkable fish chowder and grilled shrimp and scallops, while Carl stirred up a shrimp scampi in the kitchen that they all raved over. They included plenty of fresh vegetables and even a cheesecake dessert. It was declared that Emmett would have to be a permanent part of their getaways. Between him and Carl they'd blown their guests away, having been used to order out meals for the most part in the past, because Carl flatly refused to cook without help.

The rest of their two day odyssey progressed from one partner to the next. It was so damn much fun for Emmett. He never knew what he'd run across in his movements through the house. It seemed he couldn't go anywhere without encountering someone fucking a partner or getting a blow job. He even caught every one of them at one time or another simply alone in some corner, slowly jacking off.

The other side of that coin what that he was caught nearly every time he was alone with himself or partnered. The only time during that whole party that you could be fairly well guaranteed of some privacy was at night when you were alone with your chosen partner for the night.

Emmett completed that off crew with his current roommates, but let them know that they'd have to find a replacement roommate after that. Carl had one more year on his tour aboard the boat and Emmett was going to move in with him for that final year. That would leave Emmett with only one more year on his tour aboard the boat and he figured he'd be able to make living arrangements for that.

That final year of Carl's tour was more of the same. The five of them spent most of their free time together. And not just at the house. They were frequent visitors to the water park, the beaches, Waimea Falls, and the Polynesian Cultural Center. Of course there was always Waikiki for shopping and people watching.

The years in Hawaii were good ones for Emmett. Even after Carl left, he'd spend off crew time with Brad and Clay. Once he got married, Robert declined to indulge his appreciation for the male body. But the other three of them never feared for disclosure. That wasn't Robert's style. Besides, he'd have probably lost his career as well.

Emmett still got missives from Mark and Riley. Both were still stationed on the east coast of the United States. Mark was on a cruiser and Riley had finally managed to get the carrier birth he'd wanted from the beginning. Neither of them had been celibate through these years. Just enough guys were interested in exploring the male side of sex to give them enjoyment, though they admitted that they'd never really had the fulfilling sex they'd enjoyed with Emmett.

He felt so bad about it that Emmett never mentioned to either of them about the incredible luck he'd had in Hawaii. Oh he never denied having frequent sex. He just never went into much, if any, detail. Besides, it wasn't a very smart idea to give any specific details in emails that could be found and read if they weren't immediately deleted. There was also the fact that Emmett and Riley in particular were afraid of monitoring by military intelligence since they were in ratings that had top secret clearances. So none of them actually mentioned guys in their emails. It was always about the girls they were dating, but they knew the truth.

Instead of reenlisting and moving to a shore billet at his three year mark onboard, Emmett chose to remain on the submarine for his final year of military service. By this time, he was an E-6, or petty officer first class. His pay had jumped to nearly twenty-two hundred dollars a month.

He'd garnered a fine education in nuclear power plant operation and by the time his obligation ended, he'd have four full years of operational experience under his belt. Both were marketable qualities in the civilian nuclear power industry. He'd done some research online and discovered that reactor operators in civilian nuclear were paid very, very, very well.

Clay and Brad had moved on to new boats or shore duty by this time, so Emmett was back to being alone in his sex life. Not that it really bothered him all that much. The years in Navy schools and the close association with his four compatriots had given him more than enough time to fully explore himself and become completely comfortable with his sexual orientation. It wasn't really about the sex anymore. It was much more about the relationships. It was about the close friendships that just happened to include sex between males.

That last year of onboard time wasn't one where he was looking for new companions. He was plenty busy with his duties as Engineering Watch Supervisor, division administrative petty officer and the Engineer's Logroom Yoeman, the job that had been Carl's until his departure. Carl had, in fact, been the one to recommend Emmett for the position since he'd spent so much time in the logroom with him. Not all their time had been spent in fun. Emmett really had learned all the duties and responsibilities, so he'd been a natural for the position. The Engineer had embraced the suggestion enthusiastically since it meant he wouldn't have to break in a new man unfamiliar with the procedures.

That's not to say that there weren't some interesting encounters during that final year. Being one of the senior most petty officers onboard gave him a certain notoriety among the crew. He was the man the new guys invariably came to with questions about the engineering spaces for their ship's qualifications.

By this time, Emmett had qualified and stood watch as an Engineering Watch Supervisor. That was a position that required him to have a very well rounded knowledge of all the systems aft of frame eighty-five, the forward most reactor compartment wall. He'd roam all the engineering spaces during his six hour watch, monitoring procedures in progress, helping lower enlisted with qualifications and generally being the legs for the engineering officer of the watch, who was required to spend the majority of his time in the maneuvering room, where the reactor, electric plant and throttles were controlled.

The young men new to the boat found Emmett amazingly easy to approach and question. He always made a bit of time to help whomever asked. It was never an imposition to him. This made him amazingly popular throughout the boat. Besides, he enjoyed it. Getting to spend a bit of time in the presence of young nubile males was never much of an imposition. Even if he never got to touch, he could always dream during his alone times. That was enough.

There were two interesting encounters during that last year that were memorable to him, however. The first involved one of the cooks. A young twenty year old blond boy named Ward Nielson. It was always worth the extra time to pass the time with the cooks as they were preparing meals, because it meant Emmett could get a bit of a gawk at Ward.

It was obvious that the boy spent time developing his body. It was very well proportioned and just toned enough to interest Emmett. He knew this because the cooks typically worked in just their t-shirts. Ward's always seemed to be just one or two sizes too small because they fit so snuggly to his chest, back and abdomen. Not much that you had to imagine about that young body.

It was also clear that the boy was packing well in his pants. The bulge there was ever present. And that was saying something because Emmett had seen him a time or two going from the showers to his bunk in nothing but his underwear and he was always wearing boxers. The bulge was just as evident in just his boxers. So it wasn't that the boy was sporting a perpetual semi-erect cock. It was simply big.

The boy was also a lot of fun to be around. He seldom was in anything but a very good mood. It was obvious that he enjoyed the work he was doing. It was truly rare to find Ward irritated. Oh, and it didn't hurt that the boy really was a good cook. Many of the younger cooks when they came onboard weren't totally committed to their chosen career. The senior cooks were frequently having to keep a close eye on their efforts to ensure meals were not burnt. But not with Ward. It was the one thing all the senior cooks agreed on; Ward was dedicated to ensuring only the very best foods came out of his pots and pans.

They were about half way through this particular patrol cycle and Emmett was just a touch restless all the time. He would have to endure only one more patrol before he could muster out of the Navy and try his hand at being a civilian once again. Only a little more than six months and he'd be free of the military. It was something to think about. He'd signed his recruitment papers at age nineteen, but because of the delay in his actual oath-taking and departure for boot camp, he was twenty by the time he was officially in the Navy.

Here he was, five and a half years later, nearly twenty-six. Sometimes he felt much older. Especially when the new men came aboard for their first tour on an operational Naval submarine. They all seemed so much younger. Many were still in their goofy late teen stage. Boot camp hadn't *quite* knocked all that teenage angst out of them.

As it happened, Ward and Emmett shared the same sleeping cube. But, since they worked different watch sections, Emmett had never had occasion to see Ward changing in the cube. Ward was always gone by the time Emmett returned to the cube.

This one day, however, Emmett hadn't had much to do after watch. His log room duties were up to date, so he'd only had to spend a couple of hours updating some miscellaneous records and catch up a bit of correspondence for the Engineer. He went all the way forward this particular morning to grab a cup of coffee and simply sit in the crew's mess to unwind. The morning cook was already there starting to pull his menu together.

"Hey Emmett," greeted Russell, the first class petty officer that usually handled the morning and lunch meals.

"Hey Russ," replied Emmett warmly. "Going solo this morning?" It was unusual to see just one cook in the galley. But then, his assistant, Ward, was probably in the cooler, pulling together ingredients.

"Not supposed to be. I'm not sure what's happened to Ward. He's usually waiting for me when I arrive."

"Well, we sleep in the same cube, want me to go see what's keeping him?"

"I was just getting ready to call the Chief of the Watch in control and ask him to send a runner back to roust the boy. But if you wouldn't mind, I'd just as soon not let the powers know that he's late. Can't remember the last time the boy wasn't on time."

"Hey, it's no problem. I'll just run back and give him a shake and then come back for my morning coffee."

"Thanks. I'll warm up a couple of Danish for you in return."

"Ooh, I'm going to have to make this my morning task from now on if that's the way you're going to treat me," he laughed as he walked aft.

The cube was dark, except for the small bit of light that got in through the gap between the top of the naugahyde curtain and the door header. Not that the light was all that bright outside the cubes. The lighting in this area of the boat was subdued purposely because it was the crew's primary birthing area. But the light that seeped in was sufficient to navigate the confines of the cube.

The bunks were three high, the bottom one being only a few inches above floor level. Ward's bunk was one of the center bunks, which put it right at Emmett's waist as he stepped up to it. The naugahyde curtain across the length of the bunk were shut tight, so that meant that Ward was still inside. He tended to leave his curtains open slightly when he wasn't in it.

Emmett simply reached into the bunk where the curtains separated in the middle. His hand landed on the boy's hip. That relieved Emmett. He hadn't properly considered his action and could have ended up with his hand in the middle of the poor boy's crotch. 'Gees, Emmett,' he thought, 'You really need to stop and think before you just jump ahead.'

Well, since he'd been lucky, he leaned over so that his mouth was near where Ward's head would be and gave his hip a bit of a shake. "Hey Ward," he whispered, "Time to get your ass out of the rack. Russ could use a little help with breakfast."

"Mmrrhhh?" was the muffled reply. But that was accompanied by the boy rolling onto his back. That little move put his erect cock right into Emmett's hand.

Later, when he had time to review the event, Emmett couldn't for the life of him figure why he didn't jerk his hand away. All he could decide was that he'd been tired from the long watch and then the few hours spent in the log room. Not that it really mattered…he didn't pull away.

What he felt in his hand was not the fabric of underwear being pushed into his hand by a morning hard-on. This was raw, naked flesh. The thing was obviously sticking out the fly of his underwear. Lord it was huge. Just as large as Emmett had imagined it would be.

He had to get control of himself and this situation before he got himself into trouble. But the moment he decided that he had to pull away, Ward pushed his crotch up into Emmett's hand…several times.

Oh Christ, what was he about to let himself in for? He knew that he really shouldn't take advantage, but fuck, that cock felt so hot and so incredibly hard. What finally decided him was when he heard the whispered request.

"Please Emmett," begged Ward. To make it absolutely clear that he knew what he was asking, Ward slipped his hand under the curtain and searched about until he found Emmett's growing crotch and held his hand there, rubbing just slightly.

To say that this was unexpected, would have been an understatement. But the old saying was, 'he who hesitates is lost'. So Emmett gave in and wrapped his fist around that monster cock. At the same time, he pushed the curtain ever so slightly open; just enough so that what little light there was would give him a view of what he was holding.

What he saw was a very thick, nine inch, uncircumcised cock. He knew it was uncut, because there was still foreskin covering half of the glans despite the hardness of it.

Emmett took just a moment to look all about the cube to ensure that none of the other occupants were seeing what was happening. But all the curtains were tightly shut and the only sound was the rapid beating of his own heart.

Ward gave Emmett's crotch a slight squeeze. That brought Emmett's attention back to the matter in hand. He began to slowly stroke that magnificent tool. He immediately realized that Ward was horny as hell, because as his hand slipped over the glans, he found it wet as hell with precum. That must have been a mighty erotic dream he'd been wrapped in for there to be this much lubrication present already.

Emmett worked that lubrication into the palm of his hand and made sure to lubricate the length of that cock as he continued to stroke.

By this time, Ward had located the zipper of Emmett's jeans and had pulled it down and now had his hand inside Emmett's pants, rubbing his left facing erection through his boxer briefs. God how Emmett wanted to pull the front of his underwear down and let his cock out, but he didn't dare. At least this situation allowed for Ward to pull his hand back into his bunk, if it became necessary, before anyone could see what was going on. It'd simply appear that Emmett's fly was down, nothing more.

As the boy worked on Emmett's trapped cock, Emmett began to stroke with faster, firmer strokes. This got Ward moving. His hips began to thrust up to match Emmett's downward motions. The precum continued to flow so that there was more than ample lubrication to ensure there was no rough friction to cause injury.

The whole episode took only a couple of minutes, probably due to Ward's already over-excited cock from whatever dream he'd been in the middle of. But that enormous tool soon stiffened completely, growing in Emmett's hand significantly. The boy's hand quickly pulled out of Emmett's pants, back into the bunk as Ward's hips jumped up one final time and stayed airborne. It took every ounce of his willpower not to stick his head inside Ward's bunk and take the head of that cock into his mouth to receive the offering. What he settled for was sticking his second hand inside and covering the head so that the majority of the boy's cum would be collected in the palm of his hand.

Well, it was a huge explosion. Emmett knew this because he could feel his hand fill after just three pulses. He pulled his hand away and brought it to his mouth as he continued to stroke that throbbing cock. As he savored the taste of young cum, he thought that this was going to end up as one big mess for the poor kid. There seemed to be no ending to his orgasm. Jesus, how long had it been since this boy had gotten himself off?

But end it finally did. Ward's hips collapsed onto his bunk and Emmett simply continued to slowly stroke the shaft of his cock, avoiding the ultra-sensitive head of that uncut cock. When he was finally certain that Ward's cock was shrinking, Emmett gently pushed it back into the fly of the boy's boxers and removed his hand, licking the last remainder of the boy's personal lubrication from it.

Ward pulled the curtain open slightly so that he could see outside and watched with a slight grin on his face as Emmett finished his personal cleaning. When he'd finished, Ward motioned him down.

"Thanks," he whispered, ever so quietly. "That was incredible."

Emmett smiled in return. "This going to stay our secret?" he whispered back.

Ward nodded vigorously.

"Cool. Now, Russ is waiting for some help, you're late."

"Fuck!" exclaimed Ward in a slightly louder whisper. He pulled his head back into his bunk and there was considerable movement inside there. Emmett could only surmise that the boy was cleaning himself up a bit before trying to get out. Emmett simply left the cube and headed back to the mess hall, his unsatisfied cock reluctantly shrinking back towards something resembling normal proportions.

When he entered the mess hall, Russ was just coming out of the kitchen with a plate containing two Danish with an abundance of cream icing on each. He set those on a table near the kitchen entrance and then went to the coffee maker and poured two cups of coffee, returning to the table just as Emmett got there and was seating himself.

"So, did you catch the boy jacking off?" laughed Russ.

"Not that I know of. He seemed quite asleep when I shook him. Sounded like he was a bit worried you were going to be pissed."

"Nah, he's a great kid. He's never been a bit of trouble. The way he works on his parts of the menus makes me inclined to cut him a bit of slack. He's even started watching the newbies a bit. I certainly can't complain about that."

Just then, Ward came running into the mess hall. "Oh fuck, Russ, I'm so sorry."

"Don't sweat it kiddo. I can't remember the last time you were late."

"Chief's probably gonna hit me with extra duty for this."

"Nope," said Russ with a smile and a nod toward Emmett. "Your bunk mate, here, did it so the chief wouldn't have to know."

Ward looked at Emmett and there was just the slightest touch of apprehension. "Thanks, Emmett."

"Hey, no sweat. You can return the favor some time." Well, that was clearly a veiled innuendo. The question was; what would the youngster make of it?

What Emmett got was a smile and quick wink. "Ok, deal. Next time you fall asleep in the log room and might miss breakfast I'll come beat on the door."

"That works," answered Emmett as he heart skipped a beat. "I hate going to bed without breakfast."

"Can you pull the cinnamon rolls from the chiller and start baking them off?" asked Russ to Ward.

Ward hopped a bit and headed in the direction of the cool box. "On it."

"He's a good kid," said Russ as he got up with his empty cup and headed off to the kitchen.

Emmett made his way back to the missile compartment and his cube where he stripped down to his underwear and headed off for his morning shower. Newly cleaned and freshly dressed, Emmett grabbed the book he was in the middle of reading and headed back to the mess hall. He'd be early, but he'd sit off in a corner and nurse a cup of fresh coffee as he made a bit of headway in his book.

"Hey, Emmett!"

He looked up from his book to see Russ standing at the serving door with a filled plate in his hand.

"Time to wake up and eat before bed."

Emmett glanced at his watch as he jumped up and walked to the head of the line of waiting sailors. He couldn't believe he'd been reading for a full hour.

"Hey!" yelled the first man in line. This was one of the new seamen.

Russ simply stuck his head out the door as he handed the plate to Emmett. "Next time you're up at three in the morning and do a favor for the chief cook then you'll get preferential treatment too. Until then, don't you be worrying about it. Besides, Petty Officer First Class Page," he continued with emphasis on the rank, "has more time on board this tub than anyone currently aboard. With all the time he spends helping you nubs with qualifications he's earned a bit of front of the line privileges. You might remember that the next time you go bugging him for information, Seaman Richards."

Well, that got the poor kid to blushing. Emmett simply smiled kindly at the disconcerted kid as he thanked Russ for the plate and headed back to his table. As he started in on his meal he thought about what Russ had said and found it moderately satisfying that anyone would note the time he'd spent aboard and the time he spent helping with the kids' qualifications.

He was on his second mouth full when someone stepped up to the side of the table. Emmett looked up to find Richards standing there hesitantly.

"I'm sorry, Petty Officer Page."

Emmett smiled. "Don't worry about it, Blake. You get that steam plant drawing down pat yet?"

The boy smiled, realizing that Emmett wasn't going to hold his outburst against him. "I think so."

"Well, I'll be in crew's mess at the usual time this afternoon. Stop by and I'll quiz you."

"Thanks, Emmett."

Emmett simply chuckled as the kid went back to his breakfast. As he turned back to his own plate he noticed Russ looking at him as he continued to hand out plates. Russ simply smiled and winked. Emmett chuckled.

The next few days were nothing really special. Stand watch, do a bit of preventative maintenance, spend a little time in the log room and finally, read and sleep. Oh yes, and then there was the two hours before watch every other day when he'd simply sit in the crew's mess and be available to the young guys needing a bit of help with their qualifications. If no one showed up for help, he'd get two hours to do a bit of quiet reading.

It was three days after the wake up call for Ward that Emmett was sitting in the log room making a list of supplies he'd need to order when they pulled into port so that the next crew's log room yeoman wouldn't be short on supplies. It startled him when there came a knock at the door. Hell, no one was up at this hour of the ship's day unless they had watch.

He opened it to find Ward standing there with a sheepish grin on his face. That awoke Emmett's mind to the bit of conversation they'd exchanged the last time they'd seen one another. Emmett looked at his watch.

"Ok, I give up, it's much too early for me to be late for breakfast. It's also too early for you to have to even be in the chow hall, so what's up?" Emmett stepped out of the way so that Ward could enter.

"I stopped by to return a favor."

Emmett closed and locked the door and then turned to Ward. "You really don't have to, Ward. I mean, it was fun the other morning, but I don't want you to feel obligated."

"No obligation, Emmett. I've wanted to approach you before, but never had the nerve."

Well Emmett got a perplexed look at this. "How come?"

Ward chuckled. "Because Brad said you were awesome." Emmett's eyebrows rose at this. "You didn't know that Brad and I had a thing going, did you?"

"Uh, no."

"Well, don't worry about it. He swore me to secrecy. I've never told anyone, promise. He said I should corner you some day, but I could just never get the courage."

Emmett laughed as he worked past Ward and returned to his seat. "Ok, so what did you have in mind?"

"Brad said you have the most delicious cock onboard."

"I wouldn't know about that. I've never tasted it. Plus, I haven't tasted all the cocks onboard."

They laughed together at this. But Ward put action to words as they laughed and knelt down and began undoing Emmett's pants. Well that was direct enough. Emmett simply leaned back into his chair and lifted his ass when Ward began to pull down his pants and briefs.

There hadn't been any real time to get excited about this unexpected encounter, so Emmett was quite limp when his cock came into view.

"Oh fuck, yeah," breathed Ward. He didn't even try to work it to an erection, he lifted Emmett's limp piece of meat and swallowed it whole. He loved the feel of a guy's cock growing in his mouth.

Emmett closed his eyes and reached down and worked his fingers into the black curls, not trying to control anything that Ward did, just to have that added feeling of connection to his partner. Emmett was very pleased and very impressed. This boy knew exactly what he was about here. The touch of his lips was feather light as he slowly worked up and down on Emmett's rapidly growing member. His tongue was a marvelous appendage of delight as it stroked and massaged the glans, occasionally pausing to try and work its way into the tiny little slit at the tip that was far too small to accept it.

When Ward reached up and began to tease the underside of Emmett's scrotum with just his fingertips and fingernails, the older man's cock jumped and swelled to full size.

"Oh yeah, Ward," whispered Emmett. He'd long ago learned that he couldn't allow himself to get carried away even here. There *was* a watch stander in these spaces after all. And now that Brad had transferred off the boat, there was no one in this space that could cover for any unusual noises. Still, the amazing feelings being brought on by the boy's methods required some sort of response.

"Oh shit, Ward. You keep that up much longer and I'm going to explode."

Ward simply nodded his head, but he never slowed. In fact, he picked up his speed just a bit. Well, that was fine. Ward *did* have to be in the kitchen shortly, so there wasn't time to spare for anything prolonged. So Emmett simply let the feelings build as they would, instead of trying to dampen them.

He did manage to hold out for another minute or two, but finally it became too much and he just had to fire away. "Here it comes, baby," he whispered harshly.

His butt actually came off the chair as he jutted up at the moment of release. Oh hell yeah, he thought. This boy knew exactly what he was doing.

Ward was thrilled when Emmett moaned for him. He definitely liked hearing his partner express his delight. And when

Emmett said he was close, Ward knew that he'd done himself proud. For despite the older man's experience, Ward had managed to excite him quickly. Oh, this wasn't as satisfying as being alone where they could take all night, but for the snatch and grab circumstances onboard a submarine it was delightful and exciting. A little illicit sexual contact right under the very noses of the one who'd most object.

When Emmett's cock grew and his hips thrust up toward him, Ward was prepared. He followed the hips up, maintaining a firm hold with his lips on the head of Emmett's cock. Brad had said that Emmett was capable of overflowing his partner's mouth when he was truly excited, and Ward didn't want to miss a drop.

He hadn't dared approach anyone during this entire patrol. That's why he'd taken the unexpected chance that morning when he realized who was waking him and where his hand was. He thought about that morning wake up all that day, his mind in a state of complete shock that he'd actually tried…and succeeded in getting Emmett's interest.

The first volley, though totally expected, still overwhelmed him slightly as it slammed right past his tongue into the back of his throat. All subsequent blasts landed on his tongue allowing him to savor the taste. But that first blast had been so violent that it had nearly rocked him.

He now understood completely what Brad had meant. It took considerable effort on his part to swallow fast enough to stay ahead of the onslaught and still be able to taste the marvelous fluids filling his mouth.

When the blasts stopped and the final oozing began, Ward reached up and grasped the base of Emmett's cock and slowly, but firmly, milked all of the remaining material from inside that long tube. When he finally decided that he'd gotten all there was to get, he released his hold and allowed that magnificent penis to gently fall from his mouth. He leaned back and sat on his heals as he waited for Emmett to regain his composure.

There was a huge smile on Emmett's face when he finally lifted his head, still breathing deeply. "Whoa, kiddo, that was great.

Now my question is, do we have enough time for me to get an offering from you? That taste of you the other morning was intoxicating, but I'd really like to be able to get it directly from the source."

Ward looked at his watch and then back at Emmett. "It'll have to be quick, Emmett. I've only got fifteen minutes."

Emmett looked down at Ward's bulging crotch. "Well, that probably won't be a problem. You look about ready to rip the front of those jeans. We better hurry and get them down before you create a spot that will give you away." He laughed as Ward jumped to his feet and immediately started undoing his pants. It wasn't a moment later that he was pushing his pants and boxers down and his engorged gland jumped up and slapped the front of his t-shirt.

Well, they knew there was no time to spare, so Emmett went right to work, swallowing about three quarters of that hot, stiff piece of male flesh and blood. Hmmm. It tasted even better than he'd thought it would. Sweet flesh, hot with desire. He felt Ward's hands land on his head, but the boy allowed Emmett to take only what he could manage. He never tried to force Emmett to swallow the whole thing, a courtesy that Emmett appreciated, because he'd never been able to learn the technique of taking a cock directly down his throat. That's why he'd always been drawn to cocks that were his own size or smaller. He couldn't even quite manage all of an eight inch dick, but it was close enough that no one ever complained.

"Oh sweet heaven," breathed Ward. "Oh hell, Emmett, I'm closer than I thought. I'm going to cum soon."

"Mm hm," was Emmett's full-mouthed reply.

So Ward simply let fly, just as Emmett had done. He knew that he'd never had the power behind an orgasm that he'd just experienced with Emmett, but the volume was equal. So he groaned softly as that first burst escaped and his legs stiffened.

'Oh, such sweet necter,' thought Emmett as that first puddle bounced onto his tongue. Yeah, a blasting cock was a lot of fun to watch, but when you were more interested in consuming that slippery substance, the less violent orgasms were always preferred. It was obvious as he came that Ward wasn't being denied any pleasure. As

Emmett held the boy's ass, he could feel the quivering of the body in his hands.

"Uh...uh...uh," said Ward quietly over and over again as he released his sweet, white cream into that wet, hot orifice. God, what an experience this was.

It was a long, strong orgasm and the volume of silky, white goodness was as satisfying as Emmett could ever have hoped for. And the taste was even better directly from the faucet. Much hotter and silkier than the other morning. Of course, maybe that was just his imagination.

When the convulsions finally ended and Ward's cock began to lose its hardness, Emmett slowly pulled his head back with his lips tightly around the young man's cock and let his lips audibly smack when they pulled off the end. That got a slight chuckle out of Ward, despite his heavy breathing.

As he continued to breath, Emmett pulled the boy's pants and underwear up and buttoned them to hold them in place, leaving the final touches to Ward. Then he reached down and stood up, pulling his own clothes back into place. By the time, Emmett was back in a presentable condition, so was Ward.

"Damn, Emmett, Brad was right about you."

"Oh? And just what lies was my little buddy telling?"

"No lies, Emmett. He said you had one hot damn mouth, and he wasn't kidding. I was always raving about his blow jobs, and he kept telling me that he learned all his best stuff from you." He stepped up and hugged Emmett. "That was fucking out of this world. Thanks." He then leaned back and looked Emmett in the eyes. "Now, was it as good from the source?"

"Oh no," smiled Emmett. "It was loads better from the fountain. Thanks for stopping by this morning."

"Oh, I think you can expect a couple more visits before we pull into port, mister Petty Officer First Class Page. Can't have the most senior member of the crew feeling neglected." He laughed. "You wouldn't believe how many people have heard about Russ' little speech. You know, I don't think anybody really realized how long you've been onboard. Russ had the yeoman look it up; almost four full years."

"No big deal, really. I just don't plan to make this a career. I'm due for my enlistment to be up in seven months. Not long enough for them to justify sending me to a shore billet. I want to go make the big bucks at a commercial nuke plant."

Ward took a moment to look himself over to ensure he was presentable as he continued. "Well, I think you can expect some of the new guys to be a bit more in awe. But then, they're pretty easy to impress," he teased finally.

"All right, smart ass, get out of here and get to work. I expect something good for dessert now that I've had the main course." He stopped Ward just before he opened the door. "Thanks for coming down this morning."

"You're welcome. I'll be back again." And with that he left and started climbing the ladder.

'Funny boy,' thought Emmett as he closed the door. 'Fuck that was fun.' It had been even more spectacular because it had been so unexpected. There was a lot to be said for spontaneity. He smiled as he returned to his chair and his list of supplies. That was something he'd never expected from Ward.

When he entered the chow hall an hour and a half later, standing in line like everyone else, Ward met him at the serving window and simply smiled as Emmett selected from the offered dishes.

Ward visited Emmett four more times during the remainder of that patrol. They were fun times, but they did not continue on Emmett's final patrol because Ward had fallen in love with a girl during that off crew and they were engaged to be married at the end of the patrol. What a turn of events. Not that it mattered. Emmett was happy for him.

Emmett didn't really plan on having much time during his final patrol for extra-curricular activities anyway. He knew that he'd be busy training the two new people that'd be taking over his duties. One of those duties was as the administrative petty officer for the division. A fancy title for the guy that made sure all the records for the maintenance of the Reactor's electronic monitoring and control equipment was in perfect order.

As it happened Emmett had been responsible for that paperwork since the end of his first year on the boat. He'd shown an aptitude for administration and he'd been given free rein to reorganize the records for easy access. So if anyone was going to teach someone to continue the practice of flawless records within the Reactor Operator's Division, it had to be Emmett.

The other duty that had to be passed on was that of the log room yeoman. That wasn't nearly so difficult a task. Anyone that had spent any time in the Engineering Department could be counted as experienced, since nearly all of them had installed revisions to manuals at some time during their tours. So Emmett had simply asked around and found two men willing to volunteer for the job. He ultimately chose Joshua Taylor, a second class electrician with a year and a half remaining in his tour of duty on the boat. That would give the Engineering Officer a reliable man for a goodly time frame; long enough so that the Engineer could move on to a new assignment.

The refit period was the ideal time to train his division admin assistant since that was the time when the major maintenance and calibrations were conducted. Mitch wasn't very imaginative in putting something new together, but he could follow an established procedure like a pit bull with his teeth in his opponent's arm. Since Emmett's system was a proven winner, that was precisely what the division needed and the main reason Emmett had recommended him for the job.

Joshua Taylor was bright and energetic, and just a bit of the farm boy type. He was always so damn happy that it was almost sickening. He always claimed that it was because he was thrilled to be off the farm and away from all the bullshit. But Emmett liked him. He loved his work and it always showed in his annual performance evaluations.

He also had enough experience with manual revisions that he was able to handle all the Reactor Plant Manual revisions throughout the department on his own, while Emmett watched over

Mitch during the refit. It wasn't until the boat had finally pulled out of port that Emmett and Joshua were finally able to get together to seriously talk about the log room yeoman job.

It was happily the easiest refit Emmett had ever gone through. The reason was that the division leading petty officer, Chief Williams, and the division officer, Lieutenant J.G. Hart, excused him from any of the maintenance. They reasoned that the rest of the division needed to learn to cope without the most experienced man always standing over their shoulder. So his job during the refit was simply to stand his watches and review all the division paperwork after Mitch filed it to ensure that everything was in perfect order.

The reactor and engine room startup after refit was always a major operation and took hours to complete. The Engineering Watch Supervisor was always busy, simply because he had to constantly be on the move from one watch station to next ensuring that everyone was properly following their procedures. Emmett had expected a busy time of it as there were going to be trainees on many of the stations.

Everyone had assumed their watch stations and things were just about to take off when the Engineer and Captain stepped into the engine room and approached Emmett. With them was the next senior Engineering Watch Supervisor, his own LPO, Chief Williams.

"Petty Officer Page," said the Captain as they approached. "Please turn over your watch to Chief Williams here."

Well, one didn't argue with the Captain of the boat, especially when this one was what they referred to as a full bird captain. You see, most captains of submarines were Commanders and wore silver oak leaves on their collars. But this captain, besides being Captain of the boat, was a full Captain by rank. He wore eagles on his collars.

So Emmett went through the proper turnover briefing with his leading petty officer and followed as the Captain walked back toward the maneuvering room. When they got there the three of them, Emmett, the Captain and the Engineer, went through the 'permission to enter maneuvering' ritual. Once inside the Engineer stepped up to the Engineering Officer of the Watch, Lieutenant Camp.

"Lieutenant, you will turn over your watch to Petty Officer Page."

Emmett nearly fainted. What the fuck was going on? Oh sure, he'd sat in the big chair from time to time so that the watch officer could take a stroll through the spaces and work the kinks out of his legs. But what the hell was this? The reactor startup was a major evolution. It was always supervised by an experienced officer.

Emmett listened carefully to the turnover. When the watch was signed over to him and he signed his acknowledgement of receiving the responsibilities for the watch, the Captain explained. But first he reached up and took down the microphone and punched the selector button that would address only the engineering spaces.

"May I have you attention please, this is the Captain speaking," he said. Once he was pretty sure he had everyone's attention, he continued.

"Petty Officer Page, the Engineer thinks very highly of your performance during your four years aboard this boat. And I have to admit to being pretty impressed as well, even though I've only been in command for a year. We both feel that you have the knowledge and expertise to supervise the reactor and engine room startup. You've served this boat with distinction for four years. You've also challenged yourself and those around you to perform at the top of their game always.

"So, in recognition of your service to this boat and all those that have served during your tenure here, we are going to offer you a rare opportunity. Never, to my knowledge, has an enlisted man been given responsibility for post refit startup. We would like you to break that tradition. You've certainly earned the right." The Captain then smiled, recognizing the shocked look on Emmett's face. "Will you accept this responsibility, Petty Officer Page?"

Emmett immediately recognized the privilege he was being granted. How could he turn down such a rare opportunity? In answer to the Captain's question, Emmett held out his hand for the microphone and pressed the button that would carry his voice throughout the ship, instead of just through the engineering spaces.

"Petty Officer Page is Engineering Officer of the Watch," he announced.

What surprised him was the response that he heard coming from all over the engineering spaces, not just maneuvering. There were applause, yells and even whistles.

"The 1MC?" asked the Captain; that being the designation of the circuit Emmett had chosen to use for his announcement. But he was smiling as he asked.

"Well, sir, if I'm going to accept the responsibility for blowing us all to kingdom come, I thought it only fair to let the entire crew know."

The Captain and Engineer simply smiled, knowing Emmett's sense of humor.

"Well then, Engineering Officer of the Watch, Petty Officer First Class Page," said the Captain, "By all means, commence blowing us all to kingdom come."

"Aye, aye, sir. Commence reactor and engine room startup."

It really wasn't a challenge. During his time aboard, Emmett had spent many hours standing watches at each and every watch station in Machinery Two, the Engine Room, and Maneuvering. His knowledge of the procedures was second to none. It wasn't something that had been required of him, just something he'd done for his own self-edification. But here was where all that knowledge would come into play.

Emmett spent the next four hours issuing orders and receiving reports. At the end of it he personally placed the call to the Captain to inform him that the engineering spaces were ready for ship's deployment on patrol. Ten minutes after the call, Lieutenant Camp requested permission to entered maneuvering and relieve the Engineering Officer of the Watch.

When he'd signed over the watch, Emmett had to take a few moments to accept congratulations from the three maneuvering room watch standers and the Lieutenant.

"Damn, Petty Officer Page," said Lieutenant Camp just before Emmett left the maneuvering room, "That was a damn good job." The Lieutenant would know. He'd supervised two of these startups during his time aboard.

Well, the congratulations continued outside maneuvering as everybody in the engine room and machinery two had to shake his hand. Chief Williams refused to return the Engineering Watch Supervisor job though.

"Oh get the hell out of here. There's only two hours left. I'll finish it up. You go forward. The Engineer and Captain want to see you in the Ward Room."

When he arrived at the Ward Room, it was to find all the senior officers present and seated at the table. He looked directly at the Captain as he stood at the far end of the table. "Petty Officer Page reporting as ordered, sir," he announced, sensing that this was a formal occasion.

"At ease, Mr. Page," said the Captain seriously, then allowed himself to slip into a grin. "So, how'd it go, Petty Officer Page?"

"Startup went very well, sir. There was only one hiccup in the engine room startup when the steam flows didn't appear to be what they should, but Chief Williams quickly discovered a partially shut gauge isolation valve and we were able to proceed."

"And your maneuvering room watch standers?"

"They did well enough. The Engineer was nice enough to give me green men on the panels," he smiled at the Engineer, "So they were understandably nervous. But they performed well and only needed one or two hints along the way to keep them on track."

"Well, according to Lieutenant Camp, you accomplished the startup as well as he's ever seen it done. Congratulations, Petty Officer Page."

"Thank you, sir." He paused, but could sense that they were hoping for a bit more from him. "It was an amazing experience, sir, one that I will remember the rest of my life, I assure you." He decided that a bit of humor wouldn't go amiss as this point. "I even managed to catch one or two of my butterflies and I plan to have them mounted for posterity."

That broke the tension as all the attending officers laughed heartily.

The Captain then rose, as did every officer in the room. The Engineer, who was standing at the end of table nearest Emmett, took the one step that brought him to his side. But Emmett kept his attention focused on the Captain.

"We all heard a story last patrol about a little confrontation in crew's mess, where one of the crew reminded some people about your seniority onboard. He also reminded them of your constant availability to every member of the crew. It got the Engineer, the XO and myself to thinking. We pulled your record during off crew and were surprised to see all the commendations in your record, and your performance evaluations have been uniformly exemplary.

"So, we put our heads together and spoke with your chief and the officers that have had the privilege of working with you and we determined that you deserved a moment or two to shine in a way that was unique for an enlisted man. In return, you performed your unexpected duties with professionalism and a degree of unmatched ability. Your chief and Lieutenant have both reported that they have rarely witnessed such a smooth and flawless startup.

"So, in recognition of your accomplishment we present you with one final commendation for your records."

The Engineer proceeded to read off the commendation with words like 'unparalleled ability', 'above and beyond requirements', and 'shining example to his ship and crew'. As the commendation was handed to him, the entire group of officers, including the Captain, gave him a salute.

Well, there was moisture in his eyes as he came to full attention and returned their salute. He then looked down at the blue commendation folder in his hand as the officers returned to their seats. He then looked back at the Captain and then looked around at all the officers present.

"Thank you very much," he said softly. "That was most definitely the highlight of my time aboard."

"Emmett, you deserved it," said the Captain in a rare demonstration of familiarity, something that he was usually dead set against between officers and enlisted. "I admit that I came back a time or two and simply listened outside maneuvering. You're a natural leader. I wish we could convince you to reconsider your decision to leave the service."

Emmett smiled. This had truly been a rocking experience. Never had he imagined that he'd enjoy having that much responsibility. But he had...completely. "Perhaps the XO could make me an offer I can't refuse," he heard himself say. After a moment's consideration, he decided that he'd truly meant it too.

"Well, I have all patrol to consider it and then two months before your actual departure date to come up with something," said the XO. "If you're really serious," he added.

"Actually, I think I am." He smiled as he looked at the XO, who'd always been easy to approach and talk to. "I give you free rein to try and wow me into staying in the military."

The XO rubbed his hands together in eagerness. "Ooh, a real challenge. This'll be fun."

The Captain then got up and walked around the table and held out his hand to Emmett. "Congratulations, Petty Office Page."

"Thank you very much, sir."

After collecting hand shakes from all the assembled officers, Emmett headed straight for the crew's mess. He definitely needed to sit for a bit with a hot cup of coffee...or two...or three. Actually, what he wanted was a good stiff drink, but it was too close to departure. Besides, now that the engineering plant was up and running, the watch rotations got tighter, with fewer free hours.

He was halfway through his first cup when Russ and Ward came up and sat opposite him.

"Did you really supervise the whole startup?" asked Russ. He'd been associated with nuclear powered vessels long enough to know some of what that meant.

"Beginning to end," he smiled as he pushed the commendation folder over toward his friends. "I have you to blame, by the way."

"Me?!" asked a startled Russ. "What the hell did I do?"

"Your little speech last patrol about my longevity onboard."

He drank two cups of coffee before he decided to take himself a nap. The four hours of intense concentration had really wrung him out. When he woke after two hours, he felt truly refreshed and decided to take a bit of time for himself and go do his laundry.

The laundry room was a small affair set off in an out of the way corner of the boat so as not to disturb anyone, working or sleeping. The room contained three sets of stacked apartment style washers and dryers with front load access. Despite their size, they were still built to industrial standards so that they'd hold up to the heavy use they'd get from a crew of one hundred and twenty-five enlisted men.

When he arrived, Emmett could hear the machines already running. Disappointing. But he decided to give a look and see how far along the occupant was with his laundry. So he quietly slid the door open and was surprised to find Joshua leaned up against the wall. Of course, it wasn't the presence of Josh that surprised him, it was the exposed erection and rapid hand movements. Josh didn't realize he was being observed because he had his eyes closed. So, Emmett politely cleared his throat.

Josh froze in place as he eyes flew open. "Oh fuck," he said quietly. "Damn, Emmett, I'm sorry."

Emmett smiled and winked at his log room replacement. "No need. We all gotta do it some time." He then looked pointedly down at the seven or so inch cock Josh held. "Not bad." He then looked up at the confused expression on Josh's face. "Do me a favor. I'll leave my bag here. When you get your stuff in the dryers come grab me at crew's mess so I can start mine up. I seem to have run out of everything." He then turned to leave.

"Emmett?"

He simply looked in as he slid the door shut. "Don't sweat it. No one will know. Our secret."

He chuckled all the way to crew's mess. Poor guy. He was going to fret about that little meeting for days, Emmett knew it. Josh was all of twenty-two, but hadn't been off the farm until he'd joined the Navy at nineteen. So the poor guy was still learning about life outside the rural environment. In many ways, he was much like Bradley, with just a bit more intelligence and a much stronger drive to succeed and grow outside his rural upbringing.

Emmett had finished one cup of coffee and another chapter in his book when Josh came in, grabbed a drink and sat across from him.

"I went ahead and tossed your clothes in the washers and got them started," said Josh.

"It wasn't necessary, but thanks. So, have you gotten all the RPM updates inserted?"

Josh's eyebrows rose a bit. This was *not* the conversation he'd expected to be having. He was so thrown by the question that he couldn't answer right away. "Uh, yeah. I finished the main seawater bay this morning before startup. That was the last of them."

"Great. So, just take a break until we're at sea. We won't start attacking the mounds of component manuals until then. We'll take a week or so to just get adjusted into underway watch rotations then start hammering away at them." Josh simply continued to stare at Emmett. "Look, Josh, don't worry about it, okay?" he said softly. "You're not the first person I've caught in that particular situation. It's nobody's business."

The smile that grew on Josh's face was not the stunning one that Emmett was use to seeing. It was much more appropriate to describe it as stunned. He also shook his head in disbelief. "Thanks, Emmett," he whispered in reply.

There was silence between them for several moments as Josh finally accepted that his reputation was safe.

"So," said Josh, finally ready to more on, "How was it in the big chair this morning?"

"Fuck, Josh, it scared the shit out of me at first. But once all the officers left and I got a chance to breath…it…felt…awesome. It was like it was my fifth time doing it and not my first."

"Well, hell, Emmett, the hardest part of the plant startup is the reactor. How many times have you done a cold reactor startup?"

He had to think about it for a moment. "Uh, seven, I think."

"And how many scram recoveries?"

Emmett laughed at that. "I don't have enough fingers and toes for that number."

"Well hell, no sweat then. Once the reactor's up and running it's a cake walk from there."

"True. But you don't have to make it sound so commonplace, ya know. How many first class petty officers have you heard of being Engineering Officer for a full startup?"

"Oh hell, Emmett, I didn't mean it to sound like that. I about shit when you announced that you were the Engineering Officer of the Watch. I was sitting right where you are when I heard it and I spit bug juice all over the table."

Emmett had to laugh at that image. "Well, I think I'll go watch my laundry and read," he said standing. "I'll get with you on watch next week and we'll set up our next excursion into log room yeoman one oh one."

"Later then," said Josh.

It was hard over the next couple of days not to think about that vision of Joshua with his fist around that handsome cock, pumping like a mad man. It really did remind him of Bradley and his fine, thin, farmer's cock. That got him to thinking about how disappointed he was that Brad wasn't staying in better touch, but what the hell. It wasn't like they'd connected in anything other than sexual pleasuring one another.

The submarine pulled out of port the day after the engine room startup, so everyone was kept busy trying to adjust their sleeping schedules to accommodate the typical three watch rotation, which meant six hours on watch and twelve off. Some of that twelve was spent maintaining and repairing equipment, but usually it was time for eating, sleeping and a bit of personal time for reading, going to religious services, or simply playing personal video machines or board and card games with friends.

Emmett was fortunate to be an EWS, though. There were enough of the senior enlisted that their watch rotation was four-section; one six hour watch and eighteen hours off. By virtue of the fact that the Chiefs usually had to be available during the ship's daylight hours, Emmett got saddled with the six to midnight watch. But that was no hardship for him. Since he wasn't being involved with the regular division maintenance schedule, it allowed him plenty of freedom.

He could spend the time after watch working in the log room without any fear of being interrupted, and then he'd have breakfast and get a good sleep before getting back up at about two in the afternoon and simply occupy himself with reading.

Emmett decided to spend a good share of his off time in the log room, away from all the usual camaraderie. He cut back to once a week helping younger guys with their qualification work, trying to encourage other qualified crewmen to pick up some of that slack. He had to start backing off of his off-time support because he wasn't going to available after this patrol.

They were three days at sea before Emmett saw Josh again. He'd finished his watch and headed for the log room for a couple of hours of quiet reading. When he arrived, he found Josh already there…doing absolutely nothing, just sitting, as if waiting.

"Thought I'd catch you here after your watch," said Josh in greeting. "Lock the door, would you Emmett? I want to talk to you…privately."

Well, since it was the middle of the shipboard night, there wasn't much chance of the Engineer needing anything, and no one else came here unless invited. So Emmett locked the door and took the second chair they'd brought in for this patrol, there normally being only one chair in this tiny space.

"So, what's up?" asked Emmett, although he thought he knew where the conversation was going to go. There was only one type of conversation that might require a late night venue and locked doors.

"My curiosity," answered Josh, "That's what's up. Did you mean what you said the other day?"

"Well, since I haven't seen you since that day in the laundry, I suppose that's the conversation you're referring to. I simply meant that I'd keep the secret of your jacking off in the laundry."

"Not that part. The part where you said 'not bad'. What did you mean by that?"

"I didn't mean to shock you, Josh," he smiled. "It was just a simple observation. Most guys won't comment on another guy's body, but I don't have that problem. There's a lot of variety in male bodies out there. It's not a crime to admire one that's put together well."

"I've never had anyone say something nice about my body."

"Ah, I think I understand. It felt nice having someone compliment your body, but you're not sure about it having been a guy."

Josh stared for several moments and it was clear to Emmett that the guy was trying to make a decision about how far this conversation could go safely. "Yeah…uh, no."

Emmett signed. "Take a breath and relax, Josh. We'll slow down a minute and just take it one step at a time." Joshua nodded, although the look on his face was still showed his uncertainty. "You want to ask some delicate questions that could get you into serious trouble if anyone found out, right?"

Joshua deflated, slumping into his chair. "Yeah," he answered softly.

"All right, let me see if I can make a bit easier for you. I'll give you a simple truth, Josh. I've know several gay sailors over the years and I've never been inclined to tell anyone. Just like me catching you jacking off, it's no one's business."

"Really? You have?"

"Yes, Josh, I have. Now, does that help you with what you wanted to talk about?"

Joshua nodded. "How'd you know?"

"It doesn't matter right now. So…are you gay?"

"I…I don't know."

"You're still a virgin." Emmett said it as a statement and not a question. He'd learned over the years that people were more inclined to give an honest response if you stated it instead of asked it.

Joshua blushed, nodded and hung his head.

"Well, Josh, I'm not sure if you've looked at any criminal codes lately, but being a virgin isn't a fucking crime. Not even the UCMJ considers it criminal."

That finally got him to relax enough to chuckle.

"That's better," smiled Emmett. "So, are you a virgin with both sexes?"

"Yeah…no…maybe."

"Well that certainly clears things up," laughed Emmett softly.

Joshua took a deep breath. "I fooled around with a friend when we were thirteen. We pulled our pants down in his family's barn and jacked off together."

"You mean you jacked yourselves off or you jack each other off?"

"Ourselves."

"Well, I hate to disillusion you, but that's not really sex, Josh. That's a circle jerk and lots and lots of guys do that. So, you've never touched a naked male or female?"

Joshua shook his head in the negative.

"Ok, so here's the big question, Josh. Have you wanted to?" A nod. "A female?" A shake of the head. "A male then." A hesitant, bowed head nod.

"Well, it's not the end of the world, Josh. Like I said, I've known several gay men in my years in this man's Navy. They've managed to establish a balance that satisfied their needs and still allowed them to have the military careers they wanted. There's no reason you can't either."

"But I don't know," begged Joshua. "I'm going crazy with these feelings."

"So, what do you plan to do about it?"

There were several moments of hesitation as Joshua looked pleadingly at Emmett. "I…I want to have sex with a guy."

Emmett nodded. "That was fairly obvious."

"I…I…I want to have sex with you." There, it was out finally.

"Ok."

Joshua's mouth fell open and his eyes immediately teared up and began to leak down his cheeks. He fell back and wilted in his chair again, staring all the while at Emmett. "Why?"

"Why did I make this so hard?"

Joshua nodded.

"I'm sorry, Josh, but if I'd made the offer, it was me hitting on you. I would have been *helping* you to make your choice. The only way this could be *your* decision was for you to ask the question."

"Oh." Joshua took a deep breath and took a moment to get back his composure. "That makes sense, I guess."

"So, have you given any thought to what you'd like to do?"

Joshua nodded. "I want to watch you cum. I want to watch myself making you cum."

Emmett smiled. "That's always a very good place to start."

Joshua nearly cracked his knees as he flung himself to the floor and grabbed Emmett's knees. But the older man resisted the move to have his legs spread apart. "Emmett!" he objected.

Emmett placed his hands gently on top of Joshua's and leaned forward so that their faces were only inches apart. "Slow down, Josh," he urged softly. "Slow down." Joshua looked up at him with those begging eyes of his. "I'm not going to change my mind, Josh." He reached up with one hand and laid it gently against the younger boy's cheek. "None of this is suddenly going to be taken out of your reach. But if you rush this, you're going to be disappointed. Take your time…take it all in. Experience every little nuance so that later you can look back on this and know you'd gotten everything you could from this chance."

Joshua took a deep breath and closed his eyes, leaning slightly into the hand on his cheek. "I've wanted this for so long," he whispered.

"Yes you have. So don't cheat yourself. It's late and most unlikely that anyone will come along to interrupt us. So take your time and let your senses take it in…*all* your senses. Look at everything. Watch every move. See every reaction." Emmett reached up and gently ran his thumb over one closed eye. "Smell the endorphins and sweat. Inhale all these uniquely male odors."

He let his thumb slide over and gently rub the boy's nose. "Feel all the different textures thoroughly." His other hand gently rubbed the back of the hand beneath it. "And if you're up to it, taste the flavors that are absolutely and completely male." His thumb dropped and caressed those slightly quivering lips.

Joshua took another deep breath and sat completely back onto his feet as he opened his eyes. He was immediately captured by those earnest, honest eyes. He was mesmerized by them. He was also amazed to see just a hint of moisture forming in them. He reached up tentatively, his hand shaking, and laid his palm on Emmett's cheek and then wiped his thumb gently across one eye, forcing the moisture to release.

"Why are you crying?"

Emmett smiled. "Because I'm overwhelmed by the privilege you're granting me, Josh. To have sex with a guy, to love his body is a marvelous experience. But to be a young man's first is an experience that should never, ever be taken for granted."

Tears began to form once again in Joshua's eyes, so Emmett reached out and grabbed his shoulders and pulled the young man to him and wrapped his arms around him. Joshua immediately returned the gesture.

"You want desperately to lose part of your virginity and you've asked *me* to witness and participate. Losing any part of one's virginity is a momentous event and should never be taken for granted. I remember my first time like it was yesterday. I want you to remember your first time as a major milestone in your life, whether you decide you're gay or not. Even if you decide that you're heterosexual, after all, you should be able to look back on this moment as one you enjoyed completely…it just wasn't what you wanted for your whole life."

Emmett felt Joshua melt into the embrace.

"How do you know so much?"

Emmett began to gently rub Joshua's back and shoulders. "I've known I was gay since I was thirteen, Josh. I've had quite a few years to experiment and experience. But I've been lucky in that I had *good* people that have helped me get everything out of each experience. As a result, I've never questioned the direction of my sexual and emotional life." He pushed Joshua back so that he could look into his eyes. "That's what I want for you, Josh. But the only way you're going to be able to make your decision…to know beyond a shadow of a doubt that this is right for you, is if you take your time."

"I want…"

Emmett placed two fingers over Joshua's lips. "Shhh. I don't want a step by step discussion, Josh. Simply act on your desires. If I'm not inclined to want you to do something, I'll tell you. Now, that doesn't mean we can't talk. Ask questions if you have them, or make observations. Just don't ask permission."

Joshua hesitated for just a fraction of a second before he leaned forward and gently set his lips against Emmett's. As their lips met, Joshua moaned.

It was a tentative kiss at first…exploratory.

It was immediately obvious to Emmett that Joshua's kissing experience was limited to parental demonstrations. There was very little depth to it. So he reached one hand up and placed it against the back of Joshua's head and pushed ever so slightly, increasing the connection of their pressed lips.

Joshua got the hint immediately. And since he was discovering that this was an altogether enjoyable experience, he pressed in even further, but not so much that the inside of their lips were pressed against their teeth. It was simply a full connection.

He began to experiment a bit with this new kind of kissing. Joshua eased up on the pressure and even separated slightly, only to connect again, lightly. He did this several times, each time landing on a slightly different part of Emmett's lips.

His heart was beating so hard and fast that Joshua was certain he could feel it against the inside of his rib cage. He could feel the heat on his face, that bit of flushed feeling that indicated he was blushing. But it didn't matter. He simply allowed these things to happen and did as Emmett had suggested and simply noted them as part of the memory of this moment.

He took a chance after a minute or so of this and gently sucked Emmett's lower lip into his mouth. The older guy responded by moaning and allowed his hands to press ever so slightly harder against Joshua's head and back. When he felt this, he became completely committed to this kiss.

This was being truly connected to another human being. This was sharing more than just physical contact. This moist connection between their bodies was intoxicating, as was the smell, something Joshua only just realized was also part of the experience. There was the aroma of this body that was not his own. There was the smell of their combined breaths as their noses caressed one another.

There was also the tactile. And it wasn't just the fabric beneath his hands. Joshua could suddenly feel the flow of skin and muscle beneath his hand as their bodies moved slightly within each others' grasp. There was the texture of Emmett's hair. But more than that, there were the bumps and contusions on Emmett's scalp; something that was totally unique to every person.

All these things molded into a complete picture of the moment. Emmett was right. This was now much more than just a sexual experience. This was an event. And for Joshua, it was an event of monumental proportions.

Between one breath and the next, Joshua stopped thinking, stopped analyzing. He allowed himself to become a sponge, one that absorbed everything about this moment without stopping to think about it. It was no longer about expectations. It was about *this* moment. Not the one just past or the one to come. There was only *now*.

His anticipation drained away and was replaced by acceptance. The need to rush on to the next step vanished. It ceased being about the destination. It was completely and utterly about the journey. It was about collecting all the hundreds and thousands of moments that would eventually culminate in one cohesive memory of the entire experience.

Emmett felt it; that one defining moment when Joshua became totally committed to the experience. All the tension seemed to drain from the body in his arms as it flowed and melted into him.

The feel of the hands on his back and head as they began exploring, not simply touching. His lips parted and he began using his tongue to taste Emmett's lips. It wasn't but a moment or two before Joshua's tongue was pressing against his lips, gently probing for full access.

Here it was; the first of the many forms of virginity that most people never even considered as such. That moment when your tongue entered another human being and you allowed their tongue to enter you. It was the very first moment of sharing body fluids, the first sharing of flesh in an intimate way. It was more than a symbolic penetration.

As Emmett opened his mouth and their tongues met in that space between their teeth, separated only by their joined lips, Joshua groaned. Emmett was amazed, really, at the profound tenderness of this first moment of touching. Joshua didn't stab at or try to battle with Emmett's tongue. He caressed it. He tasted it. He wrapped his own tongue around it.

Emmett cracked open his eyes slightly and was immediately touched to his core at the sight of the tears flowing from Joshua's eyes. This was a boy…a young man…that was greatly moved by this moment. It was a supremely profound moment for him and he was allowing his emotions free rein.

Emmett placed both of his hands on Joshua's face and began caressing and massaging Joshua's temples as his fingers entwined themselves in his short hair. He felt both of Joshua's hands wrap themselves in his hair, grabbing firmly and pressing their faces ever to slightly tighter together. And the boy groaned again; but this time with just a slight whimper to it.

That was the moment when Joshua pulled them slight apart and simply rested his forehead against Emmett's as he took in deep breaths.

"Oh wow," was all he could think to say.

"Yeah, wow," chuckled Emmett. "Is it hot in here, or is it just me?"

"No, it's me," laughed Joshua. He then proceeded to pull his shirt and t-shirt up, out of his pants. But before he could reach up and start unbuttoning the shirt, Emmett was already there doing it for him. So he simply looked up and watched his friend's face as he concentrated on his work. What he saw thrilled him. There was a hint of hunger in that face. Not a devouring sort, just one that said this man wanted to enjoy this.

Emmett was pleased that Joshua was letting him take a more active role. It was a perfect time to demonstrate that he was willing to take it just as slowly as he'd urged Joshua to do. He unbuttoned the shirt one slow button at a time, and only after he'd undone the last button did he pull the front of the shirt open. He then laid his hands gently against the fabric of the white cotton t-shirt and began to feel his way over the farm boy's chest.

"Oh, that's nice, Josh. Very nice."

There was a hard definition to his pecs. The t-shirt was also just tight enough to reveal that the nipples on those fine pecs were sharply defined and already getting hard. He turned his hands down and ran them toward Josh's lap and immediately felt the ripples of abs that were the obvious product of dedicated effort.

"Whoa. The farm boy is a stud."

Joshua blushed at this, but smiled. He was a bit surprised at how good it felt to have this guy saying nice things about his body. He'd never really believed it could mean so much to him…but it did. It made him feel like a man. And that shocked him.

Emmett felt the sudden tensing of Josh's body and looked up. "What? Did I do something wrong?"

"No…no. I just don't understand." He reached down and took Emmett's hands in his and held them tightly to his chest. "I'm kneeling here doing something sexual with another man. I'm really doing something gay. But I feel incredibly manly all of a sudden. How come?"

"That one's not really hard to understand, Josh. Have I ever come off to you as someone who was gay?"

"Hell no. You're always so masculine."

"Yes I am. I'm a man. I just happen to prefer being intimate with other men. I'm actually not very turned on by the feminine men I've met. I want my hands to hold a man's body, not a woman in a man's body." He chuckled. "Don't get me wrong, I've spent time with a few of the feminine types. But it wasn't because of their femininity. They were just fun guys to be around. It's when I'm with a manly man that I feel the most complete though. Being able to share unrestrained masculinity with another man who is doing the same always makes the experience more intense for me…like right now."

When Joshua smiled this time, it was accompanied by a look of supreme revelation.

Emmett almost laughed, but held it back and simply smiled. "You don't have to start prancing around and swishing your hips, Josh. There is no great universal law out there that says gay men have to swish and prance and be all limp wristed. Gay men can be just as masculine as any heterosexual male."

Joshua released Emmett's hands and started removing his unbuttoned shirt while Emmett went back to his gentle exploration of his t-shirt covered chest and stomach. When his shirt was sitting in a heap on the floor, Emmett reached down and grabbed the bottom of Joshua's t-shirt and began to slowly pull it up. The abs that finally saw the light were just as defined as they'd felt. Then those pecs and ever harder nipples came into view and Emmett paused for just a moment to gently rub his thumbs over those two nubs.

Joshua sucked in a harsh breath as those thumbs caressed his nipples. His rock hard cock strained mightily against the restraining fabric of his trousers and underwear. "Oh yes," he said in a throaty whisper.

Emmett smiled at the response. Not all guys had such sensitive nipples. But it was always so much fun when they did. He gave those hard brown points a gentle squeeze and had the satisfaction of feeling and seeing Joshua stiffen beneath his hands.

All right, enough teasing for the moment. He pulled the t-shirt up, forcing Joshua to lift his arms. He pulled it off and tossed on top of the shirt. "Oh, yeah, this is a stud," he said as he ran his hand down the front of Joshua's naked torso. This boy was definitely excited. The heat radiated off his body in waves. And finally came the moment of truth; Emmett reached all the way down and slid his hand over those bulging pants and gently squeezed.

Emmett's original plan had been to let Joshua satisfy his curiosity about another male body, but decided at this moment that he'd give this uncertain boy the opportunity to really work out in his mind if this was the direction he wanted for his life. The way to do that was to get him off and then see how he reacted to the idea of returning the favor. With that in mind, Emmett squeezed his hand tighter as he pushed his chair back and lowered himself to his knees, pushing at Joshua's chest, forcing him to lean back.

He felt the trapped piece of young manhood straining, pulsing against the inside of those trousers as if it might be able to free itself if it just pushed hard enough. That meant that this poor guy was likely to be close to lift off, and Emmett couldn't allow that to happen inside his clothes.

Emmett released Joshua's crotch and began unfastening and unzipping his trousers. He didn't rush it, though. He slowly unbuttoned Joshua's pants and then equally slowly pulled the zipper down, being ever so careful not to touch the hidden treasure beneath.

Joshua was a tighty, whitey boy and those briefs were certainly stretched to their limit, trying to contain its prisoner. There was a damp spot beginning to form at where the head lay. Emmett took pity on this poor thing and he grasped the waistband of both pants and briefs and pulled them down simultaneously.

Once released, Joshua's cock slapped once, lightly, against his abs and then settled quickly, pointing straight up at Emmett. It quivered there, as if to say, 'do *me*, do *me!*' The quivering stopped immediately when Emmett reached down and cupped the finally visible nuts.

"Uhhhgggg," groaned Joshua as he thrust his hips up. "Oh damn, yeessss."

The leaking of fluids took on new proportions…a new energy. The head of his cock flared and refused to diminish. No… this would not last long, thought Emmett. Not that it mattered… not really. Right now Joshua wanted to experience an orgasm that was caused by another man. The time consuming loving could come another day. This moment was for losing his crotch-born virginity.

This was the moment for shattering the metaphorical barrier of his sexual ignorance.

"Please, Emmett," he breathed, "Don't make me wait!"

Ah, so willing…so eager. Emmett leaned down and, grabbing the base of that cock with his free hand, wrapped his lips around the flared head and licked at the accumulated fluids, savoring their glorious taste as he pushed his head down and down until his nose was buried in that respectable bush of soft hair. Joshua's hips jutted up each time Emmett bobbed down and it only took three strokes to bring him to the cusp of glory.

"Uh!...uh!...uh!!"

Joshua's hips came up one final time and stayed there as his balls pulled up tightly into his groin and he felt the final rush of his seed as it coursed the length of his manhood and burst forth, not into daylight, but into the darkness of another human's body…his mouth…his hot, moist, hungry mouth. The tingling of his body was not limited to his crotch in the normal manner. It spread this time to encompass his entire body, from his toes, to the top of his head, to the tips of his fingers.

It was a mind numbing orgasm, unlike any he'd had in his life. He knew that this would be the orgasm that would be the standard by which he'd always compare other orgasms. As his body-wracking release began to subside and he could once again think, he realized that this was his moment of epiphany. As he opened his eyes a crack and looked down into Emmett's eyes as he continued to milk Joshua's cock, it was glorious to see him there. No regrets, no doubts, no shame. This was the way intimacy was meant to be… for him.

He only had enough energy for a weak smile, but it was given with all the feeling he had. This was acceptance of what he'd felt all these years. This was the understanding of what it was that made him different. This was completely, utterly, and totally right!

When Emmett finally released him and sat up, Joshua gathered all his remaining strength and leaned up with him and kissed him, long and lingering.

Well, this was an encouraging sign, thought Emmett. This was a kiss of gratitude. This was a kiss that said, 'Yes! This is what I've always wanted!' There was nothing tentative or regretful about the way Joshua pressed his advantage. And if the kiss weren't enough of an indication of his decision, the gentle hand in Emmett's crotch put the period and exclamation point on this statement of desire and longing.

When Joshua broke the kiss, he made it abundantly clear how he wanted this encounter to end. "Stand up, Emmett, please?"

Emmett paused for just a moment to gently caress Joshua's cheek and then stood, pulling his t-shirt off and dropping it on the counter to his right, glancing back to locate the chair for possible later use.

Joshua was all smiles as he reached up with shaking hands and undid Emmett's belt and then began unbuttoning his pants. He'd noticed when he had his hand in Emmett's crotch that he wasn't hard. He wasn't completely soft, but he was nowhere near being fully erect. That made Joshua want to hurry a bit so that he could watch the process of that hardening tool. To see it up close on another male body was an exciting prospect. So he didn't play around. He got Emmett's pants undone and then pulled the pants and boxer briefs down so that he could totally enjoy the sight of a thickening cock.

No, it wasn't limp. It *was* bigger than he'd thought it would be. He'd never imagined that Emmett was hung so well. But it was far from erect. It still pointed primarily toward the floor. But there was obvious thickening taking place.

Joshua reached between Emmett's knees and grabbed the lip of the chair and pulled it toward him. "Sit down, Emmett."

Oh thank God, thought Emmett. He could cum while standing, but he much preferred to be sitting or lying down. His knees tended to buckle at the end of his orgasms and he always hated the bruises on his knees as a result of it. He gratefully took the offered seat and then spread his legs so that Joshua would have all the access he could want. He then leaned back into the chair and disposed himself to enjoy watching what Joshua had in mind.

Joshua laid his hands on Emmett's thighs, his eyes glued to his crotch. What was it Emmett had said? Let all his senses be involved in this? All right, his eyes were definitely involved. His hands were connected, feeling the building heat. What else? Smell. Well, why not? Emmett had had his face in Joshua's crotch. It couldn't be so bad.

Emmett watched as Joshua slowly leaned forward, his whole being focused on Emmett's groin. Surely he wasn't going to immediately take Emmett into his mouth? But no; he paused a fraction of an inch from his cock and balls and took in a slow, deep breath. A slow smile crept onto his face as he got that first whiff of male hormones.

Oh hell, that was a glorious aroma. It was not the sort of smell that he could put a name to, but it was very pleasant. In fact, he wanted more of it. So he leaned in and actually stuck his nose into the crease between Emmett's thigh and nut sack, feeling the slight tickling of the hair there, and took another deep dose of Emmett. Oh, this was even better than the last. This time the aroma was mixed with the very physical feeling of heat as it radiated onto his face and up his nasal cavity.

As he lingered there and inhaled his first man, he felt Emmett's cock brushing against his ear as it began to grow in earnest. He felt the body around his head quiver slightly, and he felt, as well as heard, the groan that escaped Emmett's lips. Oh fuck! This was exciting!

What else was it Emmett had said? See, smell, touch…oh yes, taste. Well, why not?! He didn't even move from where he was. Joshua simply snaked out his tongue and took a long slow lick up that crease.

"Oh, fuck, yes!" groaned Emmett.

Really?! But there was no denying the hand on the back of his head that begged Joshua for more of that. And since the taste had been quite enjoyable, he complied. He worked his face in tighter and began to really attack Emmett's body and he had the satisfaction of feeling him quiver in ecstasy and groan yet again.

That's when Joshua's senses became hyper-alert. He was suddenly aware of everything. The smell, taste and feel all became one. The sight of those pubic hairs wrapped around his nose added the perfect backdrop. And then there were to sounds. The short, quick breaths and groans as Emmett gave in to his enjoyment. The feel of the man's hands on his head. There was the feel of nuts against his left cheek and the smoother skin of Emmett's thigh against his right cheek.

It was a glorious overload of sensations. It was intoxicating. He was fucking giddy in a way that drugs and alcohol had never given him. He wanted to drown himself in this magnificent high. He actually began to think that this was even better than what Emmett had recently given him. Could that be possible? Could you actually get more enjoyment out of *giving* pleasure to another?

Joshua gave himself completely over to it. At this moment it was more important to stimulate than be stimulated. It was vital that he feel the squirming and not be the one doing the squirming.

He was aware that he could no longer feel Emmett's cock against his ear, so he glanced up and saw it laying against Emmett's stomach, stiffening and relaxing repeatedly, bouncing there, leaking precum onto his stomach and into his navel.

What would that taste like? Well, that thought could only be answered with action. So he leaned in further and licked his way from Emmett's groin up until that straining member touched his nose. He maintained contact between his tongue and Emmett's stomach as he opened his mouth as wide as he could and allowed the head of Emmett's cock to slip inside.

He closed his mouth and began licking up the precum that had accumulated in that cavity on Emmett's stomach while at the same time sucking the precum off his glans. The thought had never even occurred to him that this should be so gross, taking another man's fluids into himself. All that mattered was that he wanted to experience as much of this man as he possibly could.

The taste was unexpectedly pleasant. Hot, juicy, silky, and a mixture of sweet and salty. If the preliminary juices tasted this good, how much better would the full compliment be? Well, there was only one way to find that out. He lifted Emmett's cock with his mouth and slowly began bobbing up and down on it, taking just a bit more of the length into his mouth with each downward motion.

As he got about three quarters of it into his mouth and determined that this was all he could manage, he suddenly realized in a profound sort of way just what it was he was doing. He had a cock in his mouth. He had another man's penis in his mouth. The appendage that this man used to piss with was moving in and out of his mouth. And it was glorious!! So hard, and yet so soft at the same time.

He reached in with one hand and began massaging Emmett's nuts, wanting to involve all his body in this experience. Without even thinking about it, really, he reached up with his other hand and began rubbing at one of Emmett's nipples.

The result of all of this was that he felt that rock hard cock in his mouth harden even further. It swelled, stretching his mouth open even further.

"I'm cumming," hissed Emmett. "Watch out, Josh."

Somehow Joshua realized that he needed to pull off just a bit, so he pulled up so that just the head of Emmett's cock was in his mouth. He instinctively moved the hand from Emmett's nuts to his shaft and began jacking him off as he swirled his tongue over and around the swollen head. The first blast actually landed under his tongue, which probably save him from choking on that large initial ejection of cum.

Joshua closed his eyes and concentrated…hard. This was a completely foreign substance and the natural instinct was to reject it. But he was determined to follow Emmett's earlier example and take it all in. His nostrils flared as he breathed deeply through his nose, allowing his mouth to concentrate on other matters. Breathe, accept, swallow. Breathe, accept, swallow. It was a litany that he repeated in his head over and over again.

There was no rejection of the taste. That was even better than the precum had been. Thicker, hotter, and in greater quantities. But the vast volume of it was such that he had to work hard and fast to take it all in without gagging. It actually helped that the blasts came so rapidly. He didn't have time to really dwell on it. It was more action and reflex than conscious thought. Accept and swallow. Accept and swallow. Oh yeah…and breathe.

When he finally felt Emmett's body collapse, he slowed down and allowed the next few spurts linger on his tongue where he could savor the taste and feel. It also allowed him to breathe deeply and rapidly, catching up on the missed breaths he'd neglected to take as he was forced to swallow in rapid succession.

Cum. Sperm. Semen. Jiz. Spunk. Love juice.

There seemed to be no end to the names men had given their life giving fluid. But whatever one called it, it lay there on Joshua's tongue. As he rolled it over his tongue, the realization finally set in that he'd done it. He'd really done it.

His fantasies had come to fruition in a small room on a Navy submarine, hundreds of miles from civilization. It hadn't happened in a darkened room with a stranger. It'd happened in a well lit cubicle, where every little nuance had been arrestingly visible.

This had not been a last ditch effort to experience what his mind had conjured. This had been a crystal clear, joyful *experience*. This had been far and away the best experience of his short life. It was about someone coming to his rescue as he floundered to understand himself. It was about him taking a chance and taking charge. Even if it had turned out that he didn't like this, it would have been worth it, it would have been a day worth remembering fondly.

But he *did* like this. No…he loved it.

As he let Emmett's softened penis slip from his mouth, he laid his head against Emmett's stomach and simply surrendered to his feelings. His over-stimulated senses combined with his hypersensitive emotions and could lead to only one release. He wept quietly for a moment or two in happiness as he felt Emmett gently caress his hair.

After a minute or so, Joshua lifted his head and kissed Emmett ever so gently. "That was incredible, Emmett."

"Thank you, and you're welcome." He then looked deeply into the younger man's eyes for several moments. "So…you've made your decision." It was a statement, not a question, because there wasn't a whole lot of doubt about the outcome.

"Oh yes. I'm gay. I can't doubt that any longer."

"Let's pull ourselves together," suggested Emmett quietly. "I'd like to spend some time talking about all this over the next couple of months. I'm not going to be around much longer and I'd like to give you some advice, if you're willing to hear it."

"Yes, Emmett," answered Joshua as he tucked in his shirts and fastened his pants. "I have a lot of questions still."

"Good. Then we'll talk while we work in here. Now, I don't know about you, but I'm about as relaxed as I'm going to get. I need a shower and some rack time."

"Me too." He stepped up and pulled Emmett into an embrace and another kiss. "Thank you…so much."

"It's been my pleasure, Josh."

As he made his way forward and up to his birthing cube, Emmett was lost in thought. 'That was unexpected.' He was pretty sure that at some point Josh would approach him and thank him for not spreading the story of catching him jacking off. He'd never in his wildest dreams thought that Josh might be interested in experimenting with male sex though.

The young guy had really performed well, too. Emmett had never expected him to take his little speech to heart. But he'd gotten himself right into the experience. He'd overloaded himself with sensory input. He'd looked, touched, smelled and even tasted to the fullest extent possible. It'd all resulted in an extraordinary blowjob for Emmett.

What he'd originally thought would be a final patrol with no opportunities for sex, was quickly shaping up to be one that would entail a crash course in the do's and don'ts for a new, emerging gay military man.

It had been an easy prospect with Mark back in 'A' School because they'd had nearly six months to allow Mark to properly explore his sexuality. There'd been no need to educate anyone since then. All his partners had been well established in their sexuality by the time he'd come across them. But here he was again with a young man that could easily get himself discovered if he didn't understand himself and what he projected to the world around him.

That would be Emmett's task. Fortunately, his division wasn't expecting him to really be involved in the day to day tasks. So that meant that he would have all the time he needed to fit his discussions in with Joshua's working schedule.

The next four days didn't give them any opportunities to get together and it sort of surprised Emmett that Josh didn't seek him out at every opportunity. But in fact, the young man had made quite a point of only projecting the image of their usual friendship whenever they encountered one another. It certainly boded well for the boy's future. If he could keep his sexual life well separated from his professional, especially at this early stage of his awakening, he was destined to be a relatively happy guy.

When Emmett had realized this about Josh, it got him to thinking and reflecting on his own career thus far. What was it that made him so successful at merging the two sides of his life without going mad in frustration and loneliness?

Well, part of that had been easy to answer. He'd not been lonely because he'd never really been without someone that he could share a bit of intimacy when he developed the undeniable itch. That was aided by the fact that he didn't have the insatiable drive that some men had.

Bradley, for instance, was a sex maniac. The boy seemed to have a one track mind in that regard. He was always wanting more and more. There just never seemed to any satisfying his overpowering itch. This wasn't a bad thing during the off crew periods because they could easily get away. But the patrol periods were a time for potential disaster. He'd actually sat Brad down just before the patrol and explained his own philosophy to the boy.

That was probably the single most important factor in his own success, he realized. His sex drive just wasn't out of control. It wasn't the thought that dominated his every waking moment as it seemed to be with Brad. That's not to say that he couldn't take advantage of a chance encounter if it happened. Emmett had more than a few moments of unexpected opportunity, and he'd been more than capable of rising to the occasion. Most of them had been with curious straight guys that just *had* to experience it once, or were just so overwhelmingly horny that they were more than happy to accept a bit of outside help regardless of the source.

Those had all been enjoyable and had never led to any complications. All of those little vignettes had ended exactly the same. 'Thanks, Emmett, that was great. But could we forget this ever happened?'

Emmett smiled every time he remembered one of those little moments. Some of the participants would have shocked his friends if they'd ever learned of them. Two of them had even been officers. What stories he could tell, if he was inclined to that sort of thing. But no, it'd always been about trust.

So the thing that made Emmett so successful at merging the two sides of himself was the fact that he wasn't looking for 'the one'. In fact, in reviewing his gay life, he came to the conclusion that if there'd ever been any inclination to form a permanent bond with anyone, there would have been only two choices; Theison and Mark.

He smiled as he thought of Theison. Emmett had gotten a new email from him just before leaving on this patrol. Theison was excited because he'd found someone special and they were making plans to start up a separate ranch near his parents' place; one that was still connected financially with the family business, but still separated by miles of open range.

Theison and his partner were intending to make it a ranch where gay ranch hands could find a safe, profitable environment to pursue their professional love of horses and the outdoors while still being free to let their frowned upon relationships flourish and grow. If anyone could make something like that work, it was bound to be Theison.

Mark, on the other hand, had just written to say that he'd decided to reenlist for another five year stretch.

That had been a disappointing email. And Emmett had been surprised by his disappointment. But after careful thought, he'd come to the conclusion that he'd been harboring the hope that he and Mark might meet up after their tours in the Navy and try and make a life together.

That piece of news had been what prompted Emmett to give the Executive Officer the freedom to pursue a reenlistment package that might entice Emmett to stay in the military. And the XO had taken the challenge to heart. Just yesterday he'd cornered Emmett in the passageway outside officer country and told Emmett that he'd arranged for Emmett to take the Chief's exam while they were on patrol. He'd made it clear that if Emmett could pass the exam that it'd open up a whole plethora of opportunities for him.

It was fortunate that he'd been relieved of the majority of his onboard responsibilities, because it gave him more than enough time to study the material and to get some coaching and advice from the chiefs onboard. Everyone, it seemed, was quite intent to get him to stay in the Navy.

It was a week after leaving port that Joshua and Emmett were able to arrange a time to get some of the log room backlog of work accomplished. There were half a dozen boxes stowed away containing quite a lot of revision material for the majority of the component manuals. Emmett was pulling out two of these boxes when Joshua finally arrived.

"Hey, old timer!" greeted Joshua.

"I'll give you old timer, you turd," laughed Emmett. "Here, grab this box and put it on the counter." Because the space was so small, storage always seemed to be in the most hard to reach spots. Once he was back on his feet with the second box, Emmett began opening the one in his hands.

"So, we're really going to do some honest work?" asked Joshua, and there was just the slightest hint of disappointment in his voice.

"We really need to, Josh. The Engineer is pretty easy going, but he'll check to see what progress we've been making."

"Could we at least have a hug and kiss before we get started?"

Emmett smiled at the deceptively meek way he'd said it. "Only if you keep it to just that," he chuckled. He didn't wait for

Joshua to make the move, however, because truth be known, he wanted one just as much.

For someone with little or no kissing experience, Joshua did a fine job. They exchanged just enough tongue during this kiss to hint at what might be in the offing for later, but nothing more than that.

They worked for forty-five minutes before either of them brought up anything sexual. Until then, their discussions actually related solely to the work at hand. But finally, Joshua voiced his biggest concern about this new direction his life was taking.

"Can we talk a bit?" asked Joshua.

"Of course we can talk. But until we're done with all of these changes, let's limit it to talking." Emmett smiled over at Joshua. "What's on your mind?"

"I...I'm not sure I want to get fucked." There, it was out. It's all he'd been able to think about over the last four days.

"Then don't," said Emmett matter of factly.

"What?!"

"Don't. Josh, there's nothing that says you have to have anal sex."

"But, I thought…"

"Josh, being gay does not automatically mean you have to engage in anal sex. We're all different and enjoy different things. Make your sexual experiences with other guys what you want it to be." He paused a moment and let that sink in. "I'll admit that I enjoy a bit of anal sex from time to time, but it is not the all encompassing need that some guys have. I'm very, very particular about what I allow up there."

"Oh."

Emmett chuckled. "You've been worried that I'd want to stick my monster inside you?"

"Yeah, a bit."

"Well, I'll tell you the truth, Josh; I'd never let anything as big as my dick up my ass. Now, something the size of yours has definite possibilities, but nothing as long and wide as mine." He watched as the tension drained from the younger man's body. He patted the boy's back. "Don't worry about it, Josh. Even if you were inclined to want it, I'd never even consider it without an awful lot of preparation first."

"Preparation?"

"Yeah, stretching exercises. Slowly widening the hole so it'd be able to take it."

"I find it hard to believe that a guy could take something that big without it hurting like hell," admitted Joshua.

"Hey, buddy. Think about some of the things that have come out of that hole. If you can get something big out of there, you can learn to take it the other way. But like I said, there's nothing anywhere that says you *have* to. I'm certainly not going to ask. I'll tell you something else…even if you wanted me to, I wouldn't, simply because of where we are. That's something that should be saved for away from the boat."

They were silent for a good ten minutes as Joshua digested that bit of insight. But finally he began asking more questions.

"So, any great advice?" he asked. "You're not going to be around much longer."

"My biggest piece of advice is to make any sex onboard quick. Don't try to delay your orgasms, or his. As long as you're aboard the boat, sex needs to be quick. There is just too much potential for getting caught. When I had someone that I shared with regularly we often worked it so that when we'd get together, one or the other of us would get off, but seldom both of us. I'd get him off one time…the next time, he'd get me off."

"But we both got off…"

"Yes, we did. But it was very, very early in the ship's morning, and we were behind a locked door. But even here, we should think about keeping things quick. There is a watch stander in this part of the ship and if we start spending a lot of time in here, questions are going to start being asked."

"Ok, I can see that." He was silent for a few moments. "So, what's it like having something inside you?"

Emmett chuckled. "Just can't stop thinking about it, eh?"

Joshua's neck got beet red, which meant the boy was blushing like nobody's business. "I...it feels pretty good when I touch myself."

"Yes it does. But that's nothing compared to what it feels like to have someone else do it. I may not care for getting fucked all that much, but I'll always accept someone playing around back there."

"Doing what?"

"Are you sure you want to know?"

"Come on, Emmett, I wouldn't ask if I didn't want to know," he said as he turned in his chair to look at Emmett. "I've got to get as much information as I can during this patrol. Now that I've opened this door, I want to know all I can before you run off. I think I could get myself into trouble by not having enough information."

"That's a good plan, Josh," he answered seriously, patting the young man's knee. "Ok, here's what we'll do. I'll give you all the information you need, even if you don't actually do any of it. At least that way you'll have my experiences to guide you.

"So, let's talk about the male ass." He laughed lightly at Joshua's raised eyebrows. "You remember what it felt like to have me play with your nipples?" he asked as he turned back to his work.

"Oh God yes," answered Joshua as he took the hint and returned to his manual. "I never knew that could feel so fucking great."

"Well, a lot of guys are even more sensitive at their sphincter."

Emmett then proceeded to go into a long, clinical discussion of the typical guy's ass. He described all the things he enjoyed having done to him, from rubbing, to licking, even being finger fucked. "There is nothing better than a good prostate massage to send me into an instant orgasm."

"Prostate? What *is* that, anyway, other than someplace you can get cancer?"

Emmett then described the prostate and its function in the male sexual experience. "Of course, all this information really means nothing until you've given it a try. It's just something you'll have to experience some time to understand it."

"Ok." And there was a tone in that answer that said much more. This was confirmed by Joshua's look over his shoulder.

"You serious?" asked Emmett.

"I've got to find out if it's something I'd like, Emmett. You make it sound so great. And if I'm going to experiment, I'd prefer it was with you. I trust you."

Emmett just shook his head...not in denial, but in amazement. "All right, but not until we've gotten these two boxes of changes done."

It took them another forty-five minutes to complete the work Emmett had set for them. When the last revision was in and all the trash was properly stowed for future disposal, Joshua simply sat and looked at Emmett in expectation.

"So, you want to try this?" asked Emmett. Joshua nodded. "All right. Have you showered lately?"

"Just before I came down here."

Emmett smiled. "Good. So, here's what you're going to have to do; you're going to have to trust me."

"I do trust you."

"No, I mean really trust me. I'm going to do some things to you that you're heterosexual upbringing is going to tell you is gross. You're going to have to try and relax and at least let me try. You may not like it all, and that's just fine. All I ask is that you don't reject something without at least letting me try it on you. I promise that I won't do anything to hurt you. It's just going to feel weird at first because you've been raised to believe it's a big no-no."

"Ok, I can manage that."

"Good. So, drop your pants and underwear to your ankles and get on your knees, then simply lean over the chair." Emmett smiled at Joshua's raised eyebrows. "We can't make this all sexy, Josh. We'll have to treat this as a simple lesson. Remember, quick is the watch-word while onboard."

Joshua's response was to do as Emmett had said, while Emmett dug into his little hidden stash and pulled out a small bottle of K Y. When he turned around he was greeted by the sight of Joshua's bare ass facing him, the boy looking over his shoulder, smiling.

What a fine ass it was too. It was obvious that the boy had never done any nude sunbathing, because the thing was a white as a sheet, compared to rest of his body which was well tanned. Still, it was smooth and unblemished.

Emmett sat on the floor behind those marvelous, shining orbs and reached up and pushed Joshua's shirt up his body so that the tails wouldn't be in the way of his ass or his crotch. When the shirt was up high enough, Emmett simply laid his hands flat onto Joshua's lower back and began to gently rub him, working slowly lower.

Joshua began to relax immediately as he came to realize that Emmett wasn't going to rush this. Besides, that bit of massage felt marvelous. It wasn't at all difficult for him to remain relaxed since Emmett never rushed. He just caressed and rubbed, slowly working his way further in the southerly direction. So there was no sudden, unexpected touch.

It felt so marvelous, in fact, that when Emmett was finally rubbing his ass cheeks, Joshua was in heaven. This was not the least bit weird or gross. It was nirvana. God, how could having a guy touching his ass feel so exquisite. But it did and he simple let himself enjoy it.

Emmett was really enjoying this. Such flawless ass cheeks were rare. The only hair he'd seen thus far was just a bit of fuzz, nothing intrusive. He kneaded those orbs for several moments, basking in the feel of that unblemished young male skin beneath his hands. But he did need to move on. So he began working his thumbs under Joshua's cheeks, reaching just far enough under to be able to give a bit of attention to his perineum. That little knot just behind his nuts tightened up almost immediately as the boy moaned ever so softly at the intrusion.

But it caused Joshua to automatically spread his legs ever so slightly apart. In doing so, his cheeks spread apart and Emmett was able to get a better look at the ultimate goal; Joshua's man hole. It looked very pink, very clean, and Emmett wanted to taste it. But he didn't rush. Diving in between those mounds of flesh would have freaked the boy out.

So he worked one hand back up to Joshua's lower back and began the slow invasion of the channel that led back to that little button. He worked slowly, but was soon thumb massaging that spot just below Joshua's tailbone, right at the head of his crack.

Joshua moaned at this, raising himself just a fraction higher, forcing Emmett's thumb further into that virgin canyon. Emmett didn't hesitate. He began the slow, methodical walk down that avenue of pleasure and had Joshua really worked up by the time he reached that rose bud of delight.

Well, by the time he reached that point, Joshua had spread his legs as far as they would go in this position. That gave Emmett more than enough room to play. He slowly circled around that door of delight and waited, watching as it began to pulse and sweat.

"Oh Emmett, quit teasing," breathed Joshua. "I want to feel it. Please!"

Emmett, ever the gentleman, obliged. He ran his thumb lightly over that moist.

"Sssssss," hissed Joshua as he pushed backwards into that thumb.

With that sign of approval, Emmett leaned forward and placed his tongue at the top of Joshua's crack as he continued to massage his asshole with his thumb and fingers. Moving at a steady pace, he wetted down that entire crack as he sought out that fleshy pucker. It went relatively quickly because Joshua gave no sign of rejection. In only a moment or two, Emmett pulled his thumb down and replaced it with his tongue.

"Uhgggg," breathed Joshua as he jutted his ass even further back to bury whatever it was that was back there even deeper. He glanced quickly back and nearly fainted away when he realized it was obviously Emmett's tongue that was lighting a fire down there. "Oh, Jesus, God," he groaned as he turned his head back to the front and simply gave himself completely over to this.

'Oh fuck! How can that feel so damn good!' thought Joshua.

Emmett simply smiled as he continued his work. In a surprisingly short time, he felt Joshua's hole relax and spread open. That was his moment. He didn't hesitate; he began to slowly push his tongue at that begging little orifice, gently getting the boy used to the idea of something going in and out of him from this location.

After half a dozen little penetrations at which Joshua was able to relax more and more, allowing Emmett to dig deeper, Emmett finally ran out of tongue that would fit. By feel alone, he opened his bottle of lube and squeezed a large dollop onto two fingers and then pulled his tongue out and away, quickly replacing it with his two slicked fingers, applying pressure as he forced the KY around and inside the boy.

Once lubed, Emmett set his middle finger against Joshua's sphincter and pressed slowly forward. Emmett was shocked when the boy's asshole didn't relax slowly, but opened wide as Joshua pushed against his finger, forcing it all the way in until Emmett's fist was buried between those hot, sweaty cheeks.

But it didn't remain buried for more than a moment as Joshua began to hump the chair, forcing Emmett's finger in and out in ever increasing rhythm. Well, that was *not* what Emmett had expected, but he went with it and simply held his hand steady, moving it only enough so that it never pulled out.

After a few moments of this, as he felt that ass relax just a touch more, Emmett bent that inserted finger down just a touch and felt it slide over that tiny little bulge inside. The effect was immediate and intense. Joshua's ass clamped shut and his thrusts took on a whole new fever as he groaned and hissed and humped faster and faster.

And then it happened. He stopped dead, stiffened and groaned long and hard, though not loudly. Emmett thought his whole hand was going to get sucked inside from the way that sphincter clinched and released as Joshua came all over the floor of the room.

Emmett forced his finger to slide just slightly in and out, all the time rubbing that little button of intense delights and heard Joshua's groan grow deeper.

It lasted a good twenty or thirty seconds before Joshua collapsed and Emmett stopped moving his finger. He simply sat there behind Joshua and allowed him to regain some of his composure and strength. After about a minute of so, Emmett pressed lightly on that button once again and had the deep satisfaction of feeling Joshua shudder.

"Oh, please, Emmett," whispered Joshua, "Stop. I can't take any more."

Emmett chuckled and slowly pulled his finger from Joshua's ass and chuckled again when the boy moan in disappointment as that fullness was removed. Once his finger was out, Joshua immediately sat on his heals and rested his head on the chair.

"Oh fuck, Emmett. It's a good thing they don't teach us about that in sex ed. The girls would never get any dates."

Emmett laughed at that. "So, you ready for something bigger?"

Joshua sat up and turned around. "Uh, no, I'll have to think about that one."

"I was only kidding, Josh. Honestly, I love an imaginative finger more than a dick…most times."

"Well, I can certainly see why." He then looked under the chair he'd recently been bent over. "I never even touched myself, Emmett. I don't think I've ever cum like that before."

Emmett looked down at the mess. "By the looks of that, it's probably going to be a few days before you have anything more to give."

Joshua laughed. "Yeah, right." He then stood and began pulling his pants and such back into place. "You got anything to clean that up with?"

"Hey, I was a good boy scout. I'm always prepared."

The remainder of that final patrol was a lot of fun. Joshua and Emmett would get together a minimum of once a week. They'd take care of log room business first and then spend a bit of time taking care of personal business. At other times, they'd simply get together to talk.

Joshua was finally able to open up with someone and discuss all the feelings he'd been struggling to understand all his life. They'd discussed emotions, the image he wanted most people to see, and even spent some time on the topic of toys.

By the time that patrol ended, Joshua was so much more comfortable with himself that he felt like a new man. Emmett was pleased as well, because he was certain that he'd been able to give the young guy guidance that would permit him to be himself without endangering any sort of career, be it the military of some other direction.

As for Emmett, he'd taken the Chief's exam about halfway through patrol and by the time they pulled back into port, the results were back and he'd passed with flying colors; well above average. That so pleased the XO that Emmett knew that what came out of the officer's effort would probably be pretty hard to refuse. At least, that's what the XO claimed just before they returned to Hawaii and their off crew period.

Emmett and Joshua decided to go ahead and find a small apartment together so that Joshua could have some leisure to explore his sexuality more fully, without the rush that always accompanied their onboard sex. Their first night in their new apartment had been intense and long. They'd moved in before noon, had their belongings all situated by three and gone out to dinner early. By six that night, they were back in their new digs and lounging in the oversized tub together.

That first night had gone on for five hours. They had both cum four times before the night was through. It was a hell of a way to begin their off crew period.

Joshua calmed down after that first night and Emmett was able to give Joshua a feel for what it could be like, living with another gay man. They did most things together, but not everything. It was important for Emmett that Joshua understand that there needed to be a careful balance in any relationship. So, even though they were not officially in a relationship, they went about their lives as if they were.

It was actually a good thing for Emmett as well. He'd had many good sexual partnerships over the years, but had never really given any thought to what a relationship might really involve. So the two months living with Joshua in their simulated marital bliss gave Emmett the perspective he needed to make some crucial decisions in his own life.

The first of those was that it just might be possible to have a real relationship while in the military. But it would definitely have to be carefully orchestrated. It wasn't an insurmountable undertaking though. But he also learned that it wasn't a driving need like he was afraid it might turn into. He certainly enjoyed the two months with Joshua. They'd been able to experience many things that only a couple could do. But it wasn't an absolute necessity. Emmett knew that he could be just as happy continuing his military career as he'd lived his first six years of it.

The other important thing that came out of the off crew was his decision about his potential military career. It took the XO three weeks before he had what he thought was the ultimate reenlistment package for Emmett. The meeting took place, surprisingly enough, off base, at a nice mid-range restaurant. It was a lunch meeting that was attended not only by Emmett and the XO, but also the Captain and Chief Williams.

The purpose of the lunch was made perfectly clear from the outset, but it was also made perfectly clear that lunch would take precedence. No discussion of careers and reenlistments until they were relaxing over coffee and dessert.

"Well, Mr. Page," began the XO, "I think I've managed to come up with that one reenlistment package that you won't be able to refuse."

Emmett smiled. "Well, I'm certainly all primed up to listen, sir. It's not every First Class Petty Officer that can claim to have been bribed in this fashion."

Fortunately, everyone understood that he was simply displaying his sense of humor. They all laughed.

"First off, I want you to know that the Captain got involved with this one personally," said the XO.

"I meant what I said after that startup you supervised, Mr. Page," said the Captain. "It would be a real shame to let you get away without at least trying to keep you with us. You're a very rare young man. I don't know of any other young petty officer that has spent so much time bettering himself or supporting his crew the way you have. Those qualities are rare and *must* be encouraged to remain in the Navy if we are to continue having the best Navy in the world."

"Chief Williams has also had more than a little input in what we requested on your behalf," continued the XO.

Chief Williams was actually a Senior Chief, or E-8. He had nearly fifteen years in the Navy and was one of the best chief's Emmett had ever worked under.

"I've never had a division that ran as smoothly as this one, Emmett," said the Chief. "I've never had to worry about the admin and I always knew who to come to if something needed special attention. You've been the backbone of this division and I'm going to have a hard time replacing you."

"So," said the XO as he picked up the folder he'd set on the chair beside him when they'd entered. "Here's what the Navy is prepared to offer you." He opened up the folder. "First off, the Navy will give you a three year billet as an instructor at Nuclear Power School."

Well, that was a fine beginning. Shore duty assignments for nuclear trained enlisted men were normally only two years long.

"When your shore tour is complete, you'll be offered a two year Leading Petty Officer post on any class submarine you choose."

Another fine offer.

"Those are the assignment offers. Now come the more personal items. If you accept this reenlistment offer, the Navy will advance you to Chief Petty officer immediately. You'll also be given a fifty thousand dollar reenlistment bonus to be paid to you in five equal installments on the anniversary of your reenlistment beginning the day you sign your papers."

Ok, that definitely took this into the realm of nearly impossible to refuse. An E-7 with six years of service made thirty-one hundred dollars a month. That was roughly thirty-seven thousand dollars a year. Add in the ten thousand bonus and he'd be making quite a handsome income. Especially if he remained single and utilized base housing.

"Whoa," he said softly.

That brought a smile to all three faces.

"I'll tell you honestly, Emmett," said Chief Williams, "I don't ever remember hearing of a better offer in all my years. And I've heard some pretty good ones."

"What is single Chief housing like at Nuke Power School," asked Emmett, knowing full well that the man had done a recent stint there himself.

"They're unbelievable, really. Each room is a suite. There's a bedroom, living room, and pretty nice kitchen and eating area. It was built at the same time as the new school so they're only five years old and still in excellent shape. Oh, and the bathrooms actually have tubs."

"Damn, you gentlemen are making this difficult," said Emmett.

"So, I can give you a week to think about it, Mr. Page," said the XO.

"That won't be necessary, sir. I accept." He smirked as he watched all three of them raise their eyebrows. Then he laughed. "I'm sorry, sir, but I'd already decided to accept whatever offer you made, before I came here today. To have it be this offer just puts icing on my reenlistment cake."

"Well," said Chief Williams, "You'll probably be happy to know that your advancement to Chief will happen without all the usual games. You're being advanced slightly before the usual cycle and we're not prepared to do the usual Chief's initiation with you."

"Oh, you have no idea how much that breaks my heart," laughed Emmett. The games that took place during a Chief's initiation were usually just a touch on the humiliating side. Emmett wasn't going to be the least bit disappointed to have to miss out on that.

"So, Mr. Page," said the Captain, "You're serious? You accept this reenlistment package?"

"Yes, Captain," he answered quite formally, "I accept. And I appreciate all the work you three put into getting me such a fine package." He paused as he looked at all three of them. "Gees, three years at Nuke Power School. I've always wanted to try teaching full time."

Chief Williams laughed. "It really is a great job, if you like teaching. I think you will. You've spent enough time doing it on the boat. It'll just take some getting use to doing it for a group instead of one on one."

"Well, Mr. Page," said the Captain as he reached across the table to shake Emmett's hand, "Congratulations, and good luck to you."

"Thank you, Captain. Thank you very much."

The XO was next to shake his hand. "We'll do your formal advancement ceremony on Monday at morning muster. Chief Williams has volunteered to help you get properly outfitted as a new Chief Petty Officer."

With that, the XO and Captain left, leaving a copy of the reenlistment offer for Emmett.

"Damn, Chief, is this really as good an offer as I think it is?" he asked as he glanced through the papers.

"Oh, it most definitely is, Emmett. Just getting the three year Nuke School billet is over the top. But being offered your choice of submarines as LPO?...that takes this into the extraordinary. So, when would you like to go uniform shopping? And do you have enough money set aside for it?"

"Oh, yeah, that won't be a problem. My savings are over fifteen thousand. I shouldn't have any troubles."

When he got back to the apartment, he had to swear Joshua to secrecy, but just had to tell someone. When he showed Joshua the package, the boy was dumbfounded. He'd been in long enough to know that this was indeed an extraordinary offer.

And he was thrilled for his friend. If anyone deserved to be treated a bit above the norm, it was Emmett, in his opinion.

Their personal celebration that night was rowdy and long. By the time they were done, they were both sore and exhausted.

By Friday, all of his uniform purchases had been altered and all the proper insignias and stripes had been applied.

He arrived at morning muster on Monday morning wearing his usual winter working blue uniform and hat. His advancement was the last thing on the schedule for the morning, after all the role calls and typical announcements. Everyone knew something was up though, because the Captain did not usually attend the bi-weekly musters. So no one was particularly surprised when he stepped before them at the end of the announcements.

"There is one final bit of business to conduct this morning before we let you go home," announced the Captain.

"Electronics Technician First Class, Emmett Page, front and center," ordered the XO.

The Captain continued after Emmett assumed his place before him. "The majority of you all know Petty Officer Page. A lot of you have been coached through qualifications by him. And I know that you're aware that the officers and chiefs think very highly of him. What you don't know is that we have managed to coax Petty Officer Page into reenlisting for another five year tour of duty."

That brought a round of applause.

"His orders have already been cut and he will be leaving us a week from today to go and spread his expertise and experience to new enlisted men at Nuclear Power School."

That brought another round of applause.

"But we are not going to send him off to his new command without acknowledging his extraordinary contribution, not only to his boat, but to the Navy as a whole." He then looked at Emmett. "You are an extraordinary example of what the Navy is about, Petty Officer Page. Your unwavering support of your boat and your shipmates is an example that we hope everyone will attempt to attain. So, in recognition of your outstanding dedication to your fellow sailors, your submarine and the Navy, I hereby advance you to the rank of Chief Petty Officer."

There was a stunned silence for several moments and then the entire assemblage broke into wild applause. As this went on, Chief Williams stepped up with a new shirt for Emmett to don; one that had no rate or rank insignia on it.

Emmett quickly removed his shirt and put on the new one and then put the new Chief's hat on his head. Then he came to brisk attention before the Captain and gave him the smartest salute Emmett was capable of.

"Senior Chief Williams?" prompted the Captain.

The Chief stepped up in front of Emmett. "Chief Page, it is a privilege to be able to pin your first set of Chief's anchors on your collar. These were my very first anchors and I want you to wear them. I know you'll make me proud." He then attached an anchor to each of Emmett's collars, then stood back one step and saluted.

Emmett returned the salute. "Thank you, Senior Chief. I'll do my best to always be worthy of them."

The congratulations were never ending, it seemed. It took quite a while for an entire crew of one hundred and fifty officers and enlisted to shake his hand.

When the last hand had been shaken, the Navigation Chief sought him out and handed him a small computer disk.

"Congratulations, Emmett. I thought you'd like having a video record of your advancement."

"Damn, Chief Armstrong, I really appreciate this."

The Chief laughed. "The name's Craig, Emmett."

"Thanks, Craig."

The last person to approach was the XO. "Well, Chief, you're on your way," he smiled. He then handed over a manila envelope. "These are your transfer orders and your leave orders. Your leave starts next Monday and you're expected to report to Orlando two weeks later. Good luck, Chief Page."

Emmett flew home for two weeks of relaxation with his family. He didn't get to see them often enough. But they always made the most of his visits, taking time away from their jobs to dedicate the time to being a family.

But finally the day arrived and he boarded the plane for his continuing Naval career. He'd emailed Mark and Riley and had gotten congratulatory letters in return.

So now would come a new life. As a Chief Petty Officer he'd be entitled to better living conditions and more privileges. As for companions, well he just didn't really want to think about it. There was no way to plan for things like that when you were in the military. He'd simply have to take it one day at a time and grab the opportunities that came his way, just as he'd always done.

But damn, this gay sailor's journey had been a rousing success so far; there was no reason to believe that it'd be any different as the years progressed.

A Boner Book

About the Author

I spent nine years working on or serving on Naval submarines of this type. Since then, I've worked in the commercial nuclear industry, and many other short lived careers. I'm currently living in Florida, watching life proceed at its stately pace, sharing a passion for story telling.